Simon has no idea what he's doing. He just got a job as the new alpha's personal assistant, but he's lost, and finding out that one of the humans repairing the roof is his mate isn't helping, especially because he saw Simon fall on his face and heard him talk to himself.

Valentine enjoys his job. He enjoys watching Simon even more, though. He thinks Simon is adorable, even when he's talking to himself, so when he gets the opportunity to talk to him, he grabs it with both hands.

Then Simon tells him they're mates.

Valentine and Simon start dating, and everything is perfect, at least between them. Not everyone is happy for them, though, and Simon's insecurities might mean the end of their relationship. Valentine is ready to fight for it, but will that be enough?

This book is a work of fiction. Names, characters, places, and incidents either are products of the author's imagination or are used fictitiously. Any resemblance to actual events or locales or persons, living or dead, is entirely coincidental.

Valentine
Copyright © 2020 Catherine Lievens
ISBN: 978-1-4874-3067-2
Cover art by Angela Waters

Published by eXtasy Books Inc or
Devine Destinies, an imprint of eXtasy Books Inc

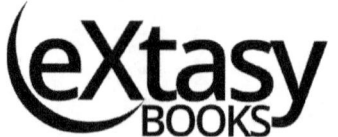

Look for us online at:
www.eXtasybooks.com or www.devinedestinies.com

Valentine
Green Hill Pride Book 3

By

Catherine Lievens

CHAPTER ONE

Simon hadn't expected to get the job. The pride was still up in the air even now that they had a new alpha, and he'd thought Gal would choose someone closer to him. Although Gal didn't have a lot of people close to him, so maybe that was the problem. He had his mate and his new beta, and also Ellery, since he'd made a show of being friendly to him, and Ellery was the mate of Gal's best friend and beta. Since none of them wanted the job, it had gone to Simon.

He also couldn't believe he'd gotten the job over Kevin. He was relieved, both for himself and for the pride. He hadn't said anything about it because it would have been mean and unprofessional, but Kevin wasn't exactly a nice person. Having him in a position of power was the last thing anyone should want. It would destroy the pride, or at the very least, the more vulnerable pride members.

"Why did you choose him?" Kevin protested.

Gal looked at him, obviously not happy, which made sense, considering Kevin's tone. "I don't have to answer to you. Why we chose Simon is a personal decision. You have no business asking."

Kevin crossed his arms over his chest. "You chose him because he knows Liam. They're friends."

Simon blinked, because that couldn't be anything further from the truth. He knew Liam, of course. Liam was a pride member. The old alpha hadn't wanted anyone in the pride to be too friendly with each other, which was why Simon didn't know him or Ellery well. Simon suspected Alpha Carter had

1

been afraid he would lose control over the pride. Whatever the case, it meant that a lot of pride members weren't close, and it was a pity. Simon wasn't friends with Liam, but he could tell Liam was a good person. He showed it when he'd become friends with Ellery, even though Ellery's father had tried to kill him.

"We're not friends," Simon quietly said. He didn't want to lose his new job because Gal would believe something Kevin said.

He should have known better. Gal looked at him, smiling, then turned his attention back to Kevin. The smile was gone in seconds. "I know what you're trying to do, and it won't work. I talked to my mate. He's not friends with either of you. The reason I chose Simon is that I think he will be the best fit. It has nothing to do with you."

"Sounds to me like it has everything to do with me if you don't think I would be a good fit."

"Kevin, please. I don't want to start a fight. I have to work with my personal assistant for hours at a time, and I need someone I know I can get along with. I'm sorry, but that's not you."

Kevin got to his feet, shaking his head. "I can't believe this. I thought things would be different now that Alpha Carter is gone, but I should have known better. You're just like him, aren't you? Playing favorites, putting your friends in powerful roles."

He didn't wait for an answer. He stomped out of the room, and they watched him leave.

Kevin was wrong. Simon knew he was. Even though Gal had asked one of his friends—an outsider—to become his beta, Simon understood why. Alpha Carter had subjugated everyone in the pride. None of them had had the guts to stand up to him, which meant they'd be terrible betas. They hadn't defended the pride when they needed to. What would happen the next time the pride was in danger?

Simon might not have worked with Gal yet, but he knew enough about him to realize he was nothing like Alpha Carter. He was surrounding himself with people he trusted, which was what every alpha should do. Alpha Carter hadn't trusted anyone. The only person he'd regularly talked to had been his beta, but that was it, and Simon was relieved that the new alpha was doing things differently. He was new in Green Hill, and it was normal for him to gather the people he trusted. He wouldn't be able to do any work otherwise.

The door slammed behind Kevin, and Simon knew he had to say something. "Thank you."

Liam turned to look at him. "What are you thanking us for?"

"For choosing me. I know Kevin was probably better for the job, but—"

"I meant it when I said I chose the person I thought was more suited for the job," Gal interrupted. "He might have been more outgoing, but that doesn't mean he was best suited. If I were you, I wouldn't think I was the second choice, because you're not. You're our first choice, and the three of us agreed on it."

Simon looked at Gal, then at Liam, and finally at Ellery. He didn't know what he'd done to earn their trust, but he was going to make sure he didn't lose it. "Still. Thank you. I know people in the pride are supposed to find jobs, but I wasn't sure I'd be able to. I don't have any kind of experience, least of all to do this job. You won't regret it."

"I know I won't." Gal gestured at the door. "I'm sure you have people you want to celebrate with. Feel free to go. You can start tomorrow."

Simon wanted to start today, but he didn't want to appear too eager, so he nodded.

His heart was still racing as he stepped out of the room.

Luckily for him and for everyone else, Kevin was nowhere to be seen. Simon had half expected him to wait outside so he could berate him some more, but he wasn't there, and Simon's steps were lighter as he headed back to the rooms his family shared.

They would be happy for him. It wasn't just because they had a new alpha. They finally were able to find a job and earn money and be independent. Kevin was correct when he'd said that being the alpha's personal assistant was a job that came with power. Simon wasn't sure what he would do with that power, but he wasn't going to wield it in a way he shouldn't. He didn't want to. The pride was his home, and he wanted it to thrive. He knew that was what Gal and his new beta were aiming for, too, and together, they could make it work.

Or at least, he hoped so.

He closed the door behind himself, not surprised to see both his parents and his sister waiting for him. They all stared at him, and he couldn't say anything. The words just wouldn't come out.

So he smiled.

Lisa — his sister and one of his best friends — squealed. She threw her arms around Simon's neck, hugging him close, almost strangling him. "I knew you could do it. You got the job, right?" She leaned back. "Please tell me I'm not doing this for nothing."

Simon laughed. Now that the stress was over, he felt relieved. "I got the job," he confirmed.

Lisa squealed again and hugged him tighter. "I'm so proud of you. I knew you would get it."

Simon hugged her back. "I wasn't sure. Kevin was there, too, and we were the last two."

She snorted and finally let Simon go so Simon's mother could hug him. "Kevin would have been an awful personal assistant. Can you imagine? He'd have tried to convince the alpha to do what *he* wanted, not what was right."

"I doubt he would have managed," Simon told her as he let go of his mom. "Gal is a good alpha. I know it might not seem like it when he's changing a lot of things, but he's truly only trying to make the pride work."

"Don't talk that way, Lisa," Simon's father said before turning his attention to Simon. "We're proud of you. You worked hard all your life, even though Alpha Carter didn't recognize it. I'm glad Alpha Brennan can see you for who you are,"

Simon smiled. He was happy about getting the job, but he was also worried that Kevin and his best friend Anne would create trouble. It wouldn't be surprising. They were trouble-makers, as the situation with Ellery had showed. Gal had to intervene, but that didn't mean they were satisfied. Simon knew better. Hell, the entire pride knew better. Kevin and Anne weren't done, and they wouldn't be until they got what they wanted. What that was, was anyone's guess.

"You should talk to the alpha if something happens," Lisa said, correctly reading Simon's expression.

He shook his head. "I don't want to appear weak." And he knew that the rest of the pride wouldn't be happy if he tattled to the new alpha. Yes, it was something he *should* do. It didn't mean he was going to do it, though.

"I think I'm going to go for a walk," he said.

Lisa clapped her hands together. "Good. That way, we can finish your cake. Jordan's busy right now, but he'll be with us later to eat it. He's going to be thrilled you got the job."

"Lisa!" Simon's mother scolded.

Simon laughed. He loved his family, and he knew that with his new job, he would be able to support them even more than he had until now. That was the only thing that mattered. Everything else, including Kevin and Anne, he could worry about later.

It was too hot, but Valentine was used to it. Working on roofs made you feel hot, and he'd been doing this job for a while. He wouldn't be doing it if he didn't enjoy it, although he had to admit that the hot weather was the thing he enjoyed the least about the job.

He straightened, rubbing his arm over his forehead, grimacing at the sheen of sweat and dust that came away from it. That wasn't a surprise, either. Roofs could only be repaired when the weather was good, which was why he and the others were working today.

He'd been stunned to find out where they would be working, and he was curious. He'd always been curious when it came to shifters, especially those who lived in Green Hill. People didn't usually see them. They kept to themselves, or at least, they had until recently. Some of them went to town now, and they'd hired Val and the others to work on the house. The roof was only the beginning, and Val couldn't wait to see what was inside.

The pride had been in Green Hill for a long time, since before Val was even born. He'd grown up being told that they were hermits, that they didn't mingle. Apparently, things had been different in the beginning, but in recent years, it had gotten worse, to the point that no one in town knew who was part of the pride and how many members it had.

Now, it was different yet again.

Val wasn't planning on asking why, but he couldn't deny he was fascinated. The thought that the people who lived in this house — the house on which he was walking — could become tigers was incredible. He was just a human, and while he wished he could have been a shifter, he also knew that being a shifter came with a lot of pain in most cases.

He heard the front door open, and he peeked down. He'd seen several people in the house earlier when he'd arrived, but even though the pride members were starting to go to town, it was still rare for Val to notice them. It was easier in pride territory, though, and he peeked, interested.

A man came out. Val didn't think he'd ever seen him—he would have remembered.

This man was gorgeous, with floppy brown hair that half hid his eyes. Val wanted to move closer and see what color the man's eyes were and if his lips looked as good from up close as they did from afar. The man was tall, but not as tall as Val, or at least, Val didn't think so. It was hard to say from a distance, though, especially with Val on the roof.

"What are you doing?"

Val turned to face his best friend, Niall. "Nothing. What do you think I'm doing?"

"I think you're drooling over that shifter."

"I wasn't drooling. I was looking at him."

"That's what I said."

Val rolled his eyes and went back to work. He couldn't deny Niall was right, though. He had been staring, and not in a bad way. He would have been staring at anyone he found attractive, but now wasn't the time or place.

"Seriously," Niall said. "Why are you staring at him?"

"Because he's gorgeous. Don't you have eyes?"

Niall grinned. "I do have eyes, and I noticed several gorgeous men around the house. Still. They're shifters."

"So? Why should that be a problem?"

"I never said it was. But you don't usually date shifters."

"I don't see how it would be different from dating a human. They might have an animal side, but it's only a part of them."

"Thank God for that. Can you imagine if we had to work on a house that was full of tigers?"

The thought made Val smile, but not for long. "You never said anything about not liking shifters."

Niall shook his head. "I don't have anything against them. I'm sure they're interesting and good people, but we still don't know them, and that has nothing to do with what they are. They're not new to town, but they never came out to talk to the people of Green Hill. There has to be a reason for that."

"I'm sure there is. It doesn't mean it's a bad reason." Just because they didn't know, it didn't mean the tigers were evil, or whatever Niall was insinuating. Val wasn't sure why he was so protective of the shifters, but he chalked it up to his fascination with them.

"You should ask him out," Niall said, surprising Val.

Val shook his head. "Why should I do that?"

"Because you find him cute."

"You're cute, too, but I never asked you on a date."

Niall grimaced. "It would be like dating my brother."

Niall and Val weren't related, but some days, it felt like it. "I can't run down there and ask him out."

"Why not? As you said, he's a cute guy, and it wouldn't be the first time you did something like that."

And he *was* cute. Val couldn't deny that.

"Just be careful, okay?" Niall added. "He might cute , but we still don't know much about the pride, so it could be dangerous. I don't want anything to happen to you."

"And you think something would happen to me if I asked him out? You're flip-flopping all over the place, Niall. Either you think I should ask him out, or you think I should stay away."

Niall stood there, thinking, and Val didn't push. He knew he couldn't, not when it came to Niall. If he did, Niall would just spout the first thing he thought of, even if it was the wrong one. He couldn't think under pressure.

Val didn't believe the cute guy or the rest of the pride was dangerous, though. He didn't know any of them except for the guy he'd talked to earlier today, but that didn't mean they were bad people. Whatever had happened, it was obvious something had changed, and they were opening themselves to Green Hill and the Green Hill inhabitants. It had to be a good thing.

Val couldn't wait to find out.

The cute guy might be a shifter, and the pride might be weird, but that didn't mean they were a danger. Val wasn't psychic or anything like that, but he didn't get those vibes from the pride, and he doubted he ever would. They were good people, a bit strange, and they were becoming part of Green Hill. Everyone should have been happy about that.

"I can see the thoughts in your brain," Niall said.

"I'm just focusing on work. Something you should do, too, before you get yelled at."

"My uncle won't care."

"Just because you're related to our boss doesn't mean you don't have to do the job. If he doesn't notice, I'll tell him. I'm not about to do your job *and* mine."

Niall pouted, but he crouched next to Val to continue working on the roof. "Fine. You win. You're no fun, though."

"Weren't you the one just telling me I was too much fun because I wanted to date a shifter?"

Niall's expression was triumphant. "So you admit you want to date him."

"I don't know. So far, I find him cute. It doesn't mean we'll mesh. He could be the worst person in the world. There's no way to know at a distance."

But for some reason, Val found himself hoping that wasn't the case. He didn't know what fascinated him so much about the cute guy who'd just left the house, but he wanted to find out. He wasn't sure he would, though. The pride might be opening up to the people who lived in Green Hill, but that didn't mean they would be happy to have one of their members date a human.

Simon was still outside when he got a call from Gal. All the pride members had Gal's phone number memorized by now, and seeing the name on the screen of his phone made his stomach churn. Had the alpha changed his mind? Maybe he'd realized that Simon would be shit at this personal assistant job. Simon hoped that wasn't the case, but he knew he had to answer. Until something changed, he was Gal's personal assistant, and his job was to answer the phone when his boss called.

"Yes?"

There was a pause, then Gal said, "Simon. I know I told you to start tomorrow, but I was wondering if you could come to my office now."

Simon's heart raced and he tried to swallow, but his mouth was dry. "Has something happened?" He wouldn't put it past Kevin and Anne to say something about him, maybe even to lie. He couldn't think of anything he'd done or said that would change Gal's mind about hiring him, but anything was possible when Anne and Kevin were involved.

"Oh, no, don't worry. I was just wondering if you might want to start looking into the stuff you'll have to do. Liam suggested it. I should have thought of it. Of course, you can wait until tomorrow to do that. I'm sure you want some free time before you start working, and I don't expect you to know everything when you start tomorrow."

Simon reached out and pressed the palm of his hand against one of the trees close by. He needed the support, because his knees felt like they were going to buckle. "I can come in right now if you want. I'm sorry. I should have suggested it myself."

"Don't apologize. You did nothing wrong. I was the one who gave you the day off. You can still have it if you want," Gal repeated.

It was tempting to say yes, but on the other hand, Simon couldn't wait. He wanted to start working and to be useful to the pride. He and Gal didn't have a relationship in any way, shape, or form, except for the fact that Gal was Simon's alpha, but Simon was eager to change that. He wanted Gal to trust him, and that would only happen if they spent time together and worked as a team. Besides, he'd been hanging around the house with nothing to do for too long. Now that Alpha Carter was gone, he wanted to start living, and apparently, that included having a job as the alpha's personal assistant. "I'll be right there," he said.

"I'm in my office. Just knock when you get here."

They hung up, and Simon hurried toward the house. He'd done what Gal has suggested, but he should probably have asked if he could start today. Did Gal think he was lazy or something like that? He hoped not. He had no idea what he was doing, but he would find out. He had to. He wanted this job, and he wanted to do it well.

He only had to hope he would be able to.

He hated Alpha Carter for not allowing him and the others to have a life. He'd kept them as prisoners, even though there hadn't been a reason. He'd made it so that none of them knew what working was like, and now they didn't have skills they could use. Simon understood how hard it was for Gal and his new beta to find them jobs. They didn't know how to do anything. They couldn't rely on the pity of the people in Green Hill, and they wouldn't want to. Still, it wasn't easy.

Simon was almost at the house when he tripped. He managed to catch himself on his hands and knees, and he looked around, grateful no one had seen him. He wasn't usually clumsy, but right now, he was overwhelmed and uneasy. He was beginning something he'd never thought he'd have, and he had no idea what he was doing. He'd have to follow Gal's instructions, but that was all he knew. He had no idea if he'd be any good at being a personal assistant. He realized the job meant he would have to talk to pride members, and, knowing some of them, they would use that to their advantage—and to his disadvantage. If he had to guess, Kevin and Anne would find a way to use his position against him and get revenge for the fact that he'd gotten the job instead of Kevin. If Simon wasn't careful, they might even try to talk to Gal, to insinuate things and make the alpha doubt his choice.

No. Simon had to be perfect, and he had to be good at the job. For himself, but also for his family, who were proud of him. For the pride that had been languishing for too long. They finally had a way to make it thrive, and Simon wanted to make it happen.

He got back to his feet and brushed his knees off. His pants were dirty, but he hoped Gal wouldn't look at his legs. He didn't exactly have a reason to.

"Come on," he told himself. "Why are you so clumsy suddenly? You can't act like this when you're with Gal." Simon felt a bit crazy talking to himself, but he'd always done it, and he wasn't going to stop now. As long as no one found out, he would be fine. It had made him feel better when he hadn't been allowed to have friends, and it was soothing, which was something he needed right now.

Someone chuckled.

Simon's blood turned to ice, and he looked around. Someone had heard him, and they were making fun of him. Even if they weren't, it had to look strange, and if the wrong person was listening in, they could report it to Gal. They could make him look like he wasn't fit for the job.

Dammit. He hadn't even lasted one entire day.

Something on the roof caught his eye, and he looked up.

He'd known there was a team of humans working there fixing the roof since no one in the house could do it, but he hadn't thought about them. He should have. One of the men was standing there, looking at him. Even from a distance, Simon could see the smile on his face. He had to have been the one who chuckled.

Simon's cheeks felt like they were on fire. He moved toward the house, ignoring the way the man was waving at him to stop. He didn't look like he was making fun of Simon, but he had laughed when Simon had fallen. Or maybe it had been when Simon was talking to himself. Simon was in a tizzy, and he had to calm down, no matter who was making fun of him. He couldn't go to work like this. Gal would realize he'd chosen the wrong person then, and he'd tell Simon to go to his room.

Simon had to make sure that when he was with Gal, he was entirely in control—calm and collected. It was what Gal deserved as an alpha. He was the face of the Green Hill pride, and Simon, as his personal assistant, was, too. He couldn't show the human on the roof how terrified he was or that he was talking to himself. The humans in town and the pride need to respect him, and that wouldn't happen if he got flustered every time he was overwhelmed. He had a chance at a new life, and he had to take it. That meant he would have to change, but that wasn't a problem. Simon had wished things were different for years. Now, he had a chance to make it happen.

He would do everything he could to do it.

Val heard the front door slam. He couldn't help but smile. He'd thought the guy was cute when he'd first seen him, but now he thought he was straight up adorable.

The guy had been talking to himself, something that

endeared him to Val. It was obvious he hadn't realized someone was watching him, and Val was sorry that he had eventually. From the way the guy ran inside, he'd been ashamed,
and Val didn't want him to be. There was nothing to be
ashamed of about falling down or even talking to yourself.
Val did it sometimes, too.

He wasn't as cute and adorable as that guy had been when
he did, though.

He shook his head. No matter what he thought of the guy,
he had to focus on the job. It was what he was being paid to
do. He was just sorry that once he would be done, he wouldn't
see the man again. Maybe he could try talking to him. He
didn't want to scare him, but it could be worth a try. Not that
he had to do it anytime soon. He and the others had been
hired for several jobs around the property, and the roof was
only the first step. It was the most important one, but there
was plenty of work to do.

"Stop daydreaming," Niall said, but Val could hear the
teasing in his voice.

"What, you can daydream and not work, and I can't?"

"That's because I'm the owner's nephew."

Val laughed. He knew Niall didn't mean anything by that.
It was true his uncle owned the company they both worked
for, but since he and Val had grown up together, the man
might as well be Val's uncle, too.

However, he wouldn't be happy with either of them if he
found out they weren't working, so Val did his best to focus
on the work. They were right on time when it was time for
them to pack up at the end of the day. They did so, and Val
yearned for a shower, a cold beer, and something to fill his
stomach.

"What are you up to tonight?" Niall asked as he and Val
climbed down from the roof, following the others. Now that
the work was over for the day, people were relaxing and

talking. A few pride members had come out to offer the team refreshments, and Val looked around. He was hoping to catch a glimpse of the man he'd noticed, but he was nowhere to be seen.

Niall elbowed him in the ribs. "You're looking for him again."

"I am."

"You're not even going to deny it?"

"Why should I?"

Niall beamed. "No reason. You're just not this obvious with your crushes usually."

"I wouldn't call it a crush. I just think he's cute."

"And you wouldn't mind getting to know him better."

"I wouldn't, no." But he doubted the same could be said for the man. He'd run inside when he saw Val on the roof, although that might have been because Val had seen him fall. Val would have no way to know, not until he talked to him. The guy wasn't here now, either, so maybe that was one more thing that pointed to him not being interested. Either that, or he was busy somewhere else.

Val was here at the pride to work, not to find himself a boyfriend. He couldn't help how cute he found the man, but he could stay away from him, at least for now. Maybe once the work was over, he could find him and ask him out. That way he wouldn't be distracted while he worked, and he would give the guy time to get over whatever had happened today.

"Do you want some lemonade?" a man asked as he walked closer. He was holding a tray with ice-cold glasses, and the sight made Val realize how parched he was.

"Thank you," he said with a smile.

The man smiled back. "You're welcome. It's the least I can do, since you didn't make us wait too long to repair the roof. Other companies wanted us to wait for months."

"That's because someone canceled a job," Niall said. He'd

taken a glass, too, and he looked like he was enjoying it.

Val took a sip of his glass, and damn, it was good. "I'm Val," he introduced himself.

"Liam. I'm the alpha mate."

Val and Niall looked at each other. They were human, but they knew what an alpha mate was. "How should we address you?"

"As Liam. I wasn't always alpha mate, and I have to admit I'm still not used to the role. Again, thank you for coming."

"Can I ask you a question?" Val said, the words crossing his lips before he could think about them.

Liam cocked his head. "Of course, although if it has to do with the roof or the house, you should probably ask my mate or Forest, the beta."

"It doesn't. I, well, I noticed a man earlier today. He went for a walk. Tallish, with messy brown hair."

Liam's smile told Val he suspected why Val was asking, but thankfully, he didn't ask. "That was probably Simon. He went for a walk earlier, after his job interview."

"Job interview?" Niall asked.

"For the alpha's personal assistant spot. He got it, and he probably needed to walk off the stress. He mentioned seeing someone on the roof when he came to Gal's office."

"Did he say anything else?" Val had to ask.

"No, but he was flustered." Liam hesitated. "You'll probably see him around the house once you start working inside. He's single, as far as I know."

Niall guffawed. Val wasn't surprised Liam had seen right through him. "Thanks for the info."

"As long as you don't make me regret it."

"I hope I won't." Val couldn't make any promises, though. He couldn't read the future.

"How about we have dinner together?" Niall asked as they headed to Val's truck. They came to work together, even though Niall had his own car.

"I don't know. I really want to shower first."

Niall made a scene of waving his hand in front of his nose. "You need to. Maybe we can meet later?"

Val had been looking forward to flopping onto his couch and not moving for the rest of the evening, but dinner didn't sound like a bad idea. He had to eat, after all, and he wasn't up for cooking. He also wasn't up for one of the frozen dinners in his freezer. "All right. Just give me time to shower, and I'll pick you up."

"Nah," Niall said, shaking his head. "I can drive to the pub. Don't worry about me. Just focus on your shower, and make it a long one. You really do need it."

Val reached out and slapped the back of Niall's head, even though he knew Niall was teasing. He didn't do it hard, and it made Niall laugh. Val ignored him and turned on the engine to drive out of the property.

"You really like that guy, don't you?" Niall asked after a while.

"I do."

"Why? You don't even know him. You never talked to him. You've only seen him from the roof, and it's not like Liam told you much about him."

"I don't know why. There's something about him, though. It made me want to climb off the roof and find him, ask him his name and if he wants to be with me."

Niall batted his lashes. "You think he would throw himself into your arms?"

"Very funny. What about you? No one's caught your eye lately?"

"No one who belongs to the pride, no. Besides, you know me. I'm not looking for a relationship the way you are. I'm a free man."

"Sure you are." Val suspected it was more because Niall

hadn't found the right person yet than because he was against it, but he didn't ask.

Niall wasn't wrong. Between the two of them, Niall was the one who had more one-night stands and boyfriends who stayed with him for only a few weeks, a month at the most. Val didn't even bother with one-night stands, not anymore. He'd had his fill of them when he was younger, and now, just like Niall had said, he wanted a relationship. He wanted to settle down, to have a home, to have someone to go back to every evening. He didn't like having an empty house, but so far, that was the only thing he had, and he would have to make do.

"And you really don't care that he's a shifter?" Niall asked, his voice more serious now.

"Why should I care?"

"I don't know. I'm not saying you should, but plenty of people would."

"Would you? If he was a guy you're interested in?"

"Hell, no. I'm pretty sure I fucked a few shifters here and there over the years. But we don't know anything about the pride. We don't know what happened in there."

"Then we'll find out."

"It's as easy as that, is it?"

Val wasn't sure it would be. There had to be a good reason the pride had stayed away from the town for all these years, and he wanted to find out what it was. He was wary of asking Simon out until he did. Maybe it was nothing, or maybe it was. Maybe there was something wrong with all the shifters in the pride.

But no. Val couldn't think like that. They were shifters, yes, but that didn't make them any different from the other shifters in town, or even from Val and Niall, even though they were human. The Green Hill pride was made up of human beings, people who were trying to open up, to become part of

Green Hill. They wanted to be part of the community, and that was a good thing. Val wouldn't start thinking they were dangerous without even knowing what had happened in the past. He had to think of them as individuals, not as a group in which everyone was the same.

Because they weren't the same. Simon was the cutest guy Val had ever seen, and he was planning on finding out whether or not they could work as a couple.

Nothing that had happened in the past would change that.

Chapter Two

Simon knew things would get better. He *hoped* they would get better, because he couldn't imagine him and Gal working together this awkwardly for the rest of their lives. Not that they would work together for the rest of their lives, of course. Simon was rushing ahead, and he shouldn't.

"Can you find me that phone number?" Gal asked.

Simon froze for a moment, then nodded. "Of course. I'll take care of it."

"Thank you." Gal barely looked at Simon, but Simon wasn't offended.

Things were weird between them, and that was okay. So far, they'd worked well together, although the fact that Simon was one of the pride members made it even weirder. He respected Gal, and he did want to work with him, but he had to relax, and it wasn't easy. Gal wasn't just judging him as his boss. He was also judging him as a pride member, and Simon wasn't sure whether he was winning that part of the challenge.

They'd been spending a lot of time together, and Gal had questions about the pride and its members. Simon always tried to answer as best as he could, but he also had to remind Gal about his meetings and calls, get the paperwork in order, and he'd been put in charge of the house renovation and the contractors. It was a lot to do, especially because he'd never had this kind of job before. Hell, he'd never had any kind of job before. He felt lost, but he did his best not to show it. He didn't want Gal to think he'd chosen the wrong person.

He moved away from Gal's desk to go back to his own office, but of course, Gal had noticed something was up. "Simon?" he called out.

Simon stopped and turned to face him. "Do you need anything else?"

Gal hesitated, then waved at the chairs on the other side of his desk. Simon bit his lower lip, but he couldn't say no to sitting there, so he obeyed, settling on the very edge of the chair as if it would help.

"You look tense," Gal said.

Simon couldn't help it — a snort escaped him. He slapped a hand over his mouth, horrified, but Gal just shook his head, smiling.

"It's okay. You don't have to check the way you talk to me. I know I'm technically your boss, but there's more to it than that."

"There is?" Simon asked.

Gal sighed and leaned back in his chair. "Maybe I should have chosen someone else as my personal assistant."

Simon paled. He'd known this was coming. "I promise I can do better," he rushed to say.

Gal shook his head. "That's not what I meant. I'm happy with the way you work, and I'm not going to find someone else. I just meant that maybe I should have chosen a personal assistant who wasn't part of the pride. You find me intimidating, right?"

Simon hadn't expected the question. He blinked, wondering how to answer. "Not intimidating, exactly."

"There *is* something, though."

"Well, you're my alpha and my boss. I respect you."

"And I'm glad for that. I respect you, too. What I meant to say is that I have a position of power when it comes to you, and it's two-fold. I'm not only your boss. I'm also your alpha, the man who decides whether or not you can be a pride member. That's a lot of power to yield over a person, and I'm starting to wonder if it was a good idea. I'm not going to ask you to quit the job or anything like that. I love working with you, even though we're still finding our way around each other. What I'm trying to say, and making a mess of it, I guess, is that you don't have to worry about me kicking you out of the pride or anything like that. Even if something happens and I decide you're not suited for the job, you're home here. You were born in Green Hill, and unless you do something horrible like trying to kill my mate, you'll always have a home with us."

He was referring to Ellery's father, who had tried to kill Liam. "I'm not going to do anything like that. For one, I like Liam."

Gal laughed. "Good, because I like him too. But you know what I mean. This was an attempt, and I'm glad we work well together, but it doesn't mean that you have to continue being my personal assistant if you don't think it fits you. I can find someone else. I can help you find another job if you want."

Simon hesitated. It was tempting to say yes, if anything because he had no idea what he was doing. He *wanted* to do this, though. He knew he could. He'd never thought he'd have this kind of life, that he'd work for the alpha, and he didn't want to lose it. "I'll stay," he said.

Gal relaxed visibly. "Good, because I'm not sure what I would have done if you had said you wished to quit. But please, let me know if something is wrong or if you have trouble of any kind. I can help you, although since I need a personal assistant, I'm sure you can imagine I'm not great with the administrative stuff. I'm grateful you're taking on a lot of things I should be taking care of, though."

"It's my job. It's what you hired me to do."

Gal slowly nodded. "Still. I realize you might not see me that way, but I'd like us to become friends. Even though I'm the alpha and your boss, I've never enjoyed being in a powerful position like this. I want people to look at me as a friend and to respect me. I don't want to be feared, and I want you to feel like you can come to me if anything happens. I've had personal assistants before, and I know it can be a tricky position."

It sounded too good to be true. Alpha Carter had stayed away from the pride members even as he scared them and ordered them around. Gal was nothing like him. He took things into his own hands if he needed to, like when Ellery had been shunned, and with Kevin and Anne, but he wasn't like Alpha Carter. Alpha Carter had guided the pride with a heavy hand, a hand that terrified the pride members. That was why they'd never gone against him. Gal, on the other hand, guided the pride with love. Every single pride member knew they could go to him if anything happened. He would take care of it, and they would be safe. Alpha Carter had been the one making the pride unsafe.

Simon swallowed. "I'm doing my best. I want to make you proud."

"You *are* making me proud. I never expected you to take over entirely from the first day. You're learning well, and so am I. You don't have to worry about your job and your home. You always have both, as long as you want them."

"Thank you."

"And thank you for taking over the contractors for the renovation. I feel I shouldn't have dropped that on you, too."

"Don't worry about it. I know the house. I've lived here all my life. Who better than me to know what needs to be done?"

"Damn right. Everything is going well, then?"

Simon opened his mouth to explain what was happening when someone knocked on the door. He and Gal looked at each other, then Gal called out, "Come in."

The door opened, and Darby peeked through. He was

about the same age as Simon, but they hadn't been friends. Alpha Carter had almost ruined the pride, and Simon decided right there and then that he needed to do something about it and bring them together.

"There's someone at the door who wants to see you, Alpha Brennan."

Gal grimaced. "Who is it?"

"One of the guys who worked on the roof?"

Gal's lips twitched. "Is that a question?"

"No. It *is* one of the guys from the roof. Anne opened the door and sent me to let you know."

Simon got to his feet. "I'll take care of it." Although he hoped Anne wouldn't still be in the entrance. She'd probably scared the poor human to death already.

"As long as you're sure. I have to make a call, but it can wait for half an hour."

"I'll do it," Simon insisted. "It's my job, and I'm in charge of the renovations."

Gal smiled at him. "You know where to find me if you need me."

Simon knew he meant it, but he hoped he wouldn't have to call him. This *was* his job, a job he'd wanted, a job he didn't want to lose. He was going to have to learn to talk to people anyway. The pride was in Green Hill, even though they hadn't actually been part of it for a long time. Things were changing, though, and so was Simon.

That didn't make him any less nervous to talk to whoever was at the door, though.

The door opened again, and Val looked up warily. A woman had opened earlier, and he hadn't liked her. He hoped she wouldn't be the one to come out this time, and he was relieved when it wasn't. He felt even better when he saw Simon, the cute guy he'd noticed from the roof. He beamed, and Simon took a step back, frowning. Val had to keep himself under check if he didn't want to freak him out.

"Yes?" Simon asked.

Val wasn't supposed to know his name, so he offered him his hand. "I'm Valentine, but you can call me Val."

Simon looked at Val's hand as if it might bite, but he slowly reached for it and took it. Val resisted the urge to link their fingers together and shook. "I'm Simon. I'm the alpha's personal assistant. Can I help you with anything?"

"Actually, yes. I wanted to talk to you for a second, or to whoever's in charge of the renovations. Would that be you?"

"It is. Alpha Brennan put me in charge once he hired me as his personal assistant." Simon looked down. "I'd like my hand back, though."

Val let go of him, but he didn't move away. He wanted Simon to realize how he felt about him, even though he wasn't sure himself.

His gaze moved behind Simon, and he noticed the woman who'd originally opened the door. She was still hovering in the entrance, staring. He didn't say anything, but he didn't miss the way Simon's back went stiff. Simon turned around to look at the woman, and the smile on his lips was forced. "Anne. Thank you for keeping Valentine company while he was waiting for me. You can go now."

Val was shocked by the expression on the woman's face. She'd been mildly interested in him, but she seemed to despise Simon. Her expression twisted, but Val had seen it, and he had no doubt Simon had, too. She was still glaring, not even trying to hide that, even though she'd toned down the hate.

"You sure you don't need anything else?" she asked, looking at Val.

"I don't. Thank you."

"Well, you should have someone else open the door next time. I'm not your maid."

She walked away, leaving both Val and Simon staring at her.

Val didn't know what to say. Since Simon was the alpha's personal assistant, he should be respected more than this woman had shown, but it was none of his business. He wanted to make it his, though, and he didn't understand why. He also didn't care. So he felt protective of Simon. Who cared why?

Simon turned his attention back to Val. "You were saying?"

"I wanted to talk about the renovations." It took Valentine a moment to remember why he was here. "We're almost done with the roof, and I wanted to know where we should go next. The alpha talked about several renovations inside the house, but we'll need someone to show them to us and explain what you want."

"He hasn't done that yet? When he hired you, I mean?"

"I don't know. I'll be honest—I'm not usually in charge. I work for a friend, and he's the one who takes on clients and jobs. But he's out sick, and he put me in charge." Niall was pissed, although not really. He kept protesting that since the boss was his uncle, he should be the one in charge, but everyone, including him, knew it would be a bad idea. He could barely make decisions for himself. What would happen if he had to make them for the business?

So Valentine was in charge, and it felt weird. He wasn't sure he liked it, although he had to admit that if it led him to Simon, maybe it wasn't so bad.

Simon looked around as if he expected the rest of the team to be there with Val. They weren't, though. They were still on the roof, finishing up and giving Val time to look around. He was grateful for that. It meant he had a few moments alone with Simon, and he wanted to make the most of it. He didn't want to seem unprofessional, though, especially not when Les had put him in charge.

"Do you want to come in?" Simon finally asked. "I can show you around and explain what's going on."

"As long as it won't be a problem with your boss."

Simon snorted delicately. "I don't see why it should be. He's new here, while I've lived in this house for my entire life. I know exactly what's broken and what needs to be fixed right away."

"It looks like I'm in great hands, then."

For some reason, that made Simon blush. He was even more adorable from up close, and Val wished he could do something. He didn't want to put the company in trouble, though. He wasn't here to flirt or to find himself a boyfriend. He was here because Les trusted him. Val had earned that trust, and he didn't want to break it.

Simon stepped to the side, gesturing at Valentine to come in. "Please."

Val obeyed and looked around. There had been talking in town about what the inside of the house was like. It was more a mansion, although since a lot of people lived here, it was normal. Val was curious, and now that he could see the inside, he felt better. "This place is huge."

"It has to be. Entire families live here."

"Jesus. I wonder how high your electric bill is."

Simon chuckled. "High enough. I was shocked when I took over the payments of the bills."

Val didn't miss the way he stayed away from him, but that was okay. It helped him resist temptation, too. "So you haven't been the alpha's personal assistant for long, right?" he asked.

"I haven't. I interviewed just the other day."

Val remembered that Liam had talked about it. "And you

like it?"

"I love it." Simon's expression softened. "I thought I wouldn't be able to do this, but I'm helping the pride." He seemed to realize he'd said too much, and his cheeks flushed again. "Anyway. Ignore my babbling. There are several spots for you to check, and I'm not sure where to start."

Val took a second to think. "Well, from what I can see, the house looks okay. Of course, since you've lived here all your life, you probably know better. What I can tell you is that we usually start with big problems, like water leaks, things like that. If there are none of those, we can look at the bathrooms and kitchen."

"We do have leaks from the roof."

"That's what I thought." Val had seen the holes in the roof when he'd fixed it, and he'd imagined there was some water damage inside the house. He'd done everything he could from outside. Now, he needed to take care of the inside. "Why don't you show me? I can tell you what needs to be done and how long it will take, and of course, the cost."

"I don't think money will be a problem." When Valentine looked at him, he shrugged. "The council is helping us. We're getting back on our feet, and they don't want us to do that alone."

Val nodded, even though he didn't fully understand. He knew what the council was, but he didn't get why they would help the pride.

Simon gestured toward the stairs. "Let's go upstairs, shall we?"

Val nodded and stepped closer. He had to walk past Simon to get to the stairs, and he made sure to brush against him. Whatever Simon was thinking, when Val got close, Simon gasped softly, and Val grinned. He wouldn't try to seduce Simon on the job, but this was a nice step forward.

Valentine — Val — was Simon's mate, and Simon didn't know what to do or say. Val didn't even turn to look at him when he gasped, something for which Simon was grateful. He tried to focus on what he was doing, but he couldn't get Val's scent out of his nose.

Val was human. Simon couldn't smell shifter on him, so he had to be. Val must know about mates, of course, since all humans knew about them by now, but that didn't tell Simon what he thought about having a shifter mate. What if he didn't want Simon? What if he didn't like shifters and didn't want to share his life with one?

Simon swallowed. He had to focus on the work. That was why Val was here and what he wanted from Simon. It would give Simon time to think things through, and hopefully, to make a decision when it came to Val.

"This way," he said, heading toward the attic. He couldn't smell Val if he stayed in front of him, but he was still hyper-aware of his presence behind him.

It was too much. Simon's life had been turned upside down since Alpha Carter had been arrested, and now he was free, he had a job, and he'd found his mate. It was overwhelming, and he didn't know how to deal with it. The best way to do that right now was to focus on the work he had to do, but that was next to impossible. How could he ignore Val's presence behind him? How could he ignore the way his tiger wanted to purr, to come out and play with the man?

Simon couldn't allow it. He still didn't know what Val would think about it, and Simon wanted to be sure before he showed him his animal side. Some humans truly didn't care, but a lot of others were wary of shifters, especially big shifters like tigers. Val didn't show any hints that he was afraid of being alone with Simon in a house full of shifters, but how was Simon supposed to know? He couldn't read minds.

"What else will there be after the attic?" Val asked as they climbed up the stairs.

Simon swallowed and tried to get his mind back on the job. "Well, I think Gal wanted to renovate the kitchen. It's been the same for decades, and now that the pride is welcoming new members, he wants it to be more practical. And of course, there are the bathrooms. All of them are private for a family or an individual, so there are a lot of them. I'll have to ask Gal. Even though I'm in charge of this project, he's the alpha."

"Of course." Val didn't look worried.

Maybe he didn't mind shifters. Maybe he wouldn't care that he was Simon's mate. Hell, maybe he'd be happy about it. Some humans could think of nothing better than being a shifter's mate. It probably felt like a fairytale or something like that, and honestly, it felt that way to Simon too right now.

Simon led Val to the attic and the problematic area. "Water started coming in a few years ago. We tried to patch it as best as we could, but none of us have experience in this. Even those who do weren't great with the roof."

Val looked around for a bit, poking and pulling, and Simon could see he wasn't happy. "I can see you tried, but it would have been better if you'd called us right away."

"We couldn't. We would have otherwise."

Val looked at Simon. He seemed curious, but he wasn't asking why they hadn't been able to call.

Simon realized that most of the town was curious. Now that Green Hill pride members were showing up in town, people wanted to know why they hadn't done that before, why they'd hidden away in the house. It wasn't a secret, so Simon didn't have a problem explaining. "Alpha Brennan only became the alpha recently. Before that, our alpha was Alpha Carter. He didn't allow any of us to go to town. He didn't want us to mingle with the town people."

Val frowned. "How come? Did he not like humans?"

"There was that, in part, but mostly, he was terrified of losing control over us. He didn't want any of us to have a job outside of the pride. He didn't want anyone from outside to come in and show us that we could have a better life. Hell, in the past few years, we weren't even allowed to go outside, even if we stayed on the property. We had to stay inside the house, and let me tell you, it wasn't fun, not with this many adult tiger shifters around." Simon snapped his mouth shut. He hadn't minded explaining the situation, but he probably should have limited himself to a shorter speech. Val wouldn't care about the details.

Or maybe he would. He was Simon's mate after all, and eventually, he would find out all about this.

Val slowly nodded. "I see. I don't think it was fair."

"It wasn't. Most of the pride members are happy he's gone."

"Did he die?"

"No. He's been arrested for trying to kidnap one of the pride members who managed to leave."

Val looked startled. "Kidnap him?"

"Yes. Cooper met his mate and left. He's not the only one who left the pride, but he was the last one, and Alpha Carter didn't take it well. I think it pushed him over the edge. He went to look for Cooper to try to bring him back, but of course, neither Cooper nor his mate would have any of that. Alpha Carter was arrested, as was his beta. That's why the pride is starting from the beginning again."

Val looked around. "That's a good thing."

"Yes."

Val nodded. "Okay. I think I've seen everything I needed to see. We should probably sit down and talk about this. Unless you want to show me the bathrooms and kitchen?"

"I certainly can if you want, but I'd rather you take care of the roof first. It's the most important job."

"I agree. All right. We can head to your office."

Simon panicked for a second at the thought of having Val so close to him, but there was no way out of it. Unless he told Val they were mates, he had to do this.

So he did.

He led Val to his office, even though it wasn't finished yet. "I apologize if it's not comfortable. Like you know, I just started this job," he said. At least there were a few chairs around the desk. They would be able to sit, and Simon would have some space.

Val looked around. "That's fine. As long as I can sit down, I'll be okay."

Simon gestured at the chairs. "Be my guest, then."

Val sat. He was still looking around, and Simon allowed him to. He needed the time to take a breather, to focus on the fact that he was doing his job right now and that he couldn't just blurt out they were mates.

"You know, I could help you fix this room," Val suddenly said.

Simon blinked. "I'm sorry?"

"Well, you said that you just started the job, and this office is obviously new. It's nice, but it doesn't have a lot of personality. I could help you. If you choose a color for the walls or something like that, I can paint them."

"I couldn't ask you to do that."

"But you wouldn't be asking me. I'm offering. If it's a problem with your boss, I can do it on my personal time, so he wouldn't have to pay me."

"Of course I'd have to pay you. If you do work, you deserve to be paid."

Val grinned. "Maybe I'm not doing this to be paid."

Simon had to swallow. "Why would you be doing it, then?"

The smile on Val's face shifted to something different,

softer, but also wicked, a smile that made Simon's insides churn. He could imagine Val sporting that smile while they were in bed together. He could imagine a life with him, even though Val didn't even know they were mates. He looked interested, though, and Simon hoped that meant they had a chance.

He didn't know what he would do otherwise. Probably panic and do something stupid.

Val didn't regret offering to spend his free time fixing Simon's office. The delight and surprise on Simon's face was reward enough, but Val was touched by the fact that Simon wanted to pay him. Simon seemed to be a good man, and it gave Val more reasons to want to get to know him.

"If you want to do this, I'll pay you." Simon paused. "It can wait, though. I don't have a lot of money. Alpha Carter didn't allow any of us to work outside of the pride. I never earned money, and even though I do now, I haven't been working long enough."

Val shook his head. "It's not a problem. I could do the job and you can pay me later, or not at all. Or I can just wait. Whatever you're most comfortable with."

Simon bit his lower lip.

Val wanted to reach out and free it, to kiss it better, but he didn't. He still didn't understand why he felt this way, but he didn't care. Whatever was up with Simon, it touched something inside Val, and he couldn't wait to see what happened next. He didn't know why he wanted to be with Simon so desperately, but he did, and he'd never been one to refuse himself this kind of thing. As long as it wasn't a one-night stand, he'd be perfectly happy.

Simon cleared his throat. "Thank you," he repeated. "We should probably talk about the attic."

"We should. I can give you an estimate of what it will cost, but when it comes to this, you need to talk to my boss. He'll be back soon. I'll call him later today to tell him what's going on so that he knows. He can approve my estimate. And I can talk to your alpha if you don't want to make that kind of decision."

"I think you should talk to him regardless. I might be in charge of the project, but he's the one who talks to the council about the money, and he should know about these things. If you can put something together, I'll show it to him."

"That's good. It would be great if you could make me a list of all the rooms we need to fix. You don't have to show them to me right away. Just put them in the order you think they should be done in, and the kind of job that needs to be done. You mentioned the kitchen?"

Simon nodded, but he seemed distracted. He was staring at Val, and while Val wasn't sure why, it made him straighten and puff out his chest. It was ridiculous. Simon had explained that this was his first job and that he'd just started, so it was obvious that he was a bit lost and didn't know what to do. It had nothing to do with Val, and the sooner Val accepted that, the better it would be, both for himself and the job. Yes, he might have a chance at something with Simon, but he had to focus on the job, not on daydreaming about Simon finding him sexy.

"I'm a tiger shifter," Simon suddenly blurted out.

Val blinked at him. "I kind of expected that, considering you're a pride member."

Simon shook his head. "What I meant is that I am a tiger shifter and that I have a mate."

Val should have known he wouldn't be lucky. The first guy he was interested in in a while, and he was mated. "I apologize if I did anything that made you feel uncomfortable," he said.

Simon shook his head. "I'm making a mess of this. What I meant is, you're my mate. I'm a tiger shifter, and I have a mate, and it's you."

Val leaned back in his chair. Simon was extremely flustered, and it was adorable. It also amused Val. The fact that Val was his mate didn't, though. It made Val feel warm inside, as if it was Christmas morning and he'd just gotten all the gifts he'd ever wanted. He hadn't thought about this when he'd dreamed of a future with Simon, but he was delighted. It also explained why he felt so drawn to Simon from the first time he'd seen him from the roof.

"Breathe," he murmured.

Simon did just that. He sucked in a deep breath, then another. "How can you be so calm?" Simon asked. "I just told you we were mates."

"I heard you. I just don't want you to faint because you're not breathing. We wouldn't be able to talk otherwise."

"You want to talk?"

"Of course I do. What did you expect I'd want to do after you told me I was your mate?"

"I don't know. I wasn't planning on telling you, not now. I wanted more time to wrap my mind around it, but it just came out."

Even though Val understood why Simon wanted to take time, he was glad he hadn't, or rather, that he hadn't seemed to be able to. "Don't worry. I won't push you. Actually, I wanted to ask you what *you* wanted."

Simon blinked. "What I want?"

"From this relationship. I mean, if you want a relationship at all. You just told me I'm your mate, but I know enough about shifters to realize it doesn't mean we have to be together."

"Is that what you want? For me to leave you alone?"

Val didn't want Simon to get the wrong impression, but he

also didn't want to come on too strongly. "No. It's not what I want. What I want is to date you. What I want is to get to know you, and hopefully, one day, to bond with you."

Simon looked stunned. "You do?"

"I do," Val confirmed. "I was attracted to you even when I didn't know you. I saw you from the roof, and I thought you were adorable."

To his surprise, Simon scowled. "I thought you were making fun of me because I'd fallen on my face and was talking to myself."

"I wasn't making fun of you. I thought you were gorgeous, and I wanted to come downstairs and help you to your feet. I wasn't laughing because I was making fun. I was laughing because you looked like my future, and I wanted nothing more than for you to know that."

Simon's eyes were wide. "You don't mince your words, do you?"

Val shrugged. "I don't see why I should. I know what I want, and if you don't want the same thing, I want to be aware of that as soon as possible. I won't force you into a relationship with me. I wasn't planning on doing that before, and I'm not planning on doing that now, either. If you want a relationship with me, I'm more than happy to oblige you. Only if you want to, though."

Simon hesitated, and Val held his breath. He wasn't lying when he said that he would give Simon all the time and space he wanted, but he couldn't deny that he wanted this desperately. He wanted Simon. He wanted to know what being with his mate was like. He wanted to share that kind of relationship, that kind of love, the sharing, and absolute trust.

But he could have those only if Simon was okay with it.

Simon finally nodded. "All right," he said.

"You're going to have to be more precise, because I have no idea what all right means," Val answered.

Simon's cheeks flushed. "I meant, all right, I want to get to know you. And to date you," he added.

Val's heart felt like it was about to explode, it was so swollen with feelings. "That's good. When would you want to go out?"

"Already?"

"We can wait to date, but I don't see why we should. We already know we're mates, and we just agreed we wanted to explore a relationship. What's making us wait?" But Val understood. So much seemed to have changed in Simon's life recently, he probably wasn't ready for this, and Val would give him as much time as he wanted.

"How does Saturday evening sound?" Simon asked instead of telling Val he needed space.

Val beamed. "It sounds perfect."

CHAPTER THREE

Now was the time for Simon to admit that he had no idea what he was doing. He'd never been on a date. He'd never had a boyfriend. He wasn't a virgin—there were too many men around his age in the pride for that to be the case. Since they'd never had anyone else, they'd experimented with each other—but it couldn't hold up to what was about to happen.

He was going on a date with his mate.

He would fuck it up. He already knew that, and he hoped Val wouldn't mind. He didn't know what he would do if Val decided he didn't have the patience to coax Simon into having a relationship with him. Besides, that wasn't the problem. Simon *wanted* a relationship with Val. They'd been texting since the first time they'd talked, and he really liked his mate.

Which was why he was even more anxious not to fuck things up.

He leaned back in his desk chair and rubbed his face. He should have been focusing on his job, but instead, he couldn't stop thinking about Val. It was Saturday, and Gal had told him he shouldn't even be working, but he'd hoped it would help. He needed to focus on something that wasn't his mate, and he'd thought work would make that happen.

He'd been wrong.

He sighed. Val would pick him up here at the house, but Simon had no idea what they were doing. Val had said he wanted to keep things simple, but what did that mean? What should Simon wear? How was he supposed to behave? He knew he had to check his teeth for spinach if they ate, but that was about all. Movies weren't real life. He couldn't rely on them to get him through this.

He sighed again and checked the time. It was only four in the afternoon, so it would be three hours before Val got here. Simon had enough time to work himself into a tizzy, and he didn't want that to happen. Bad things happened when he worked himself into a tizzy, like him falling on his face in the middle of the driveway and Val seeing him from the roof. He had to do something to distract himself, and work wasn't doing it.

He got to his feet. He wasn't hungry, but maybe a quick trip to the kitchen to get a snack would help.

He wished he hadn't had that idea once he got there. The kitchen wasn't empty, unfortunately. Kevin and Anne were there, and Simon almost left as soon as he saw them. They hadn't noticed him, but they did seconds later, and he knew he had nowhere to go.

"Here's the alpha's personal assistant," Kevin said. There was meanness in his voice, and that was enough for Simon to know he still resented him.

Simon wasn't ashamed of being Gal's personal assistant, though. Kevin was angry because he'd wanted the job and hadn't gotten it. Simon had, and he was doing a good job, or at least, he thought he was.

He straightened his back and stepped into the kitchen. "Kevin, Anne, how are you?"

Kevin snorted. "How do you think I am? You took my job away from me.

"I didn't take your job. Gal was the one who chose me. If you have anything to say, you should take it up with him."

Kevin crossed his arms over his chest. "Wouldn't you like that. That way, he'd kick me out, and you'd have everything you wanted."

Simon shook his head and moved toward the fridge. Leaving without anything would let them win, and he didn't want that to happen.

He'd always tried his best to stay away from them. He didn't like them and thought they were bullies. They weren't as bad as Alpha Carter and his beta had been, but they'd thrived on the alpha and beta's behavior, and now that they couldn't anymore, they were lost. They were still mean, still trying to control the pride members, even though they had no reason. And most pride members didn't even allow them to, not anymore. They wanted to be free, and thanks to Gal, they were. Why would they listen to Anne and Kevin?

"He's too good for us now," Anne said. "See? He's not even answering you."

"I'm not answering him because I have nothing to say," Simon explained. "I understand he's angry because I got the job, but I didn't steal anything. Gal chose, and he chose *me*. If Kevin has a problem with that, he can take it up with Gal." Simon reached to open the fridge.

Kevin stepped into his path. "Don't talk as if I'm not even there," he snapped. "You took my job away. The least you could do is look me in the eyes."

Simon sighed. This was not the best way to relax before his date. "Again, I did *not* take your job away. Gal chose the one he thought would be the best fit, and it was me. Honestly, I don't know why you thought you should get the job."

Kevin took a step back. He looked like Simon had slapped him, and Simon felt guilty for all of two seconds. Then, Kevin opened his mouth and said, "You're sleeping with him. Is that why he chose you? Because you let him fuck you?"

Simon shook his head. "He's mated to Liam. I'm *not* sleeping with him." Simon hadn't told anyone about Val, so Kevin and Anne didn't know about him yet. If things worked out, the pride would find out, and that would be okay. In the meantime, though, Simon wanted to keep it to himself. He didn't want Kevin and Anne to use Val against him.

"I know there's something there. There has to be. You're not good enough to be the alpha's personal assistant."

"It looks to me like he is," Liam said, entering the kitchen.

Simon sighed in relief. He wasn't sure how he would have gotten himself out of the situation, but he'd have found a way. He didn't want anything to ruin this day, though, and fighting with Kevin and Anne might have done just that. This way, Liam could take care of them. It might be the coward's way out, but it was also Liam's job as alpha mate.

Kevin and Anne plastered sweet smiles on their faces, but Simon — and no doubt, Liam — knew better. Liam wouldn't be fooled. He knew what they were and what they did.

"We were just talking with Simon," Kevin said.

"You were asking him if he was sleeping with my mate. Why?"

Kevin's cheeks flushed, and he looked even angrier than before. "I just thought it was strange that Gal had chosen him for the personal assistant job. That's all. We all know Simon is weird. He even talks to himself. Why would Gal want him by his side every day.?"

Liam looked at Kevin, then at Anne. "How about because he's not a bully like the two of you? Or maybe because he doesn't try to intimidate people into doing what he wants? Or even better, because he doesn't think he's owed anything. The two of you are pride members, but you're already on thin ice. You should be more careful about what you say, especially when you say it where everyone can hear you. You're lucky *I* was passing by instead of Gal. Hell, even Forest might have taken advantage of this and kicked your asses out of the pride. No one here likes you, and I don't think that's going to change if you continue to act this way. The pride has been your home for as long as it's been mine. I don't want to take it away from you, but if you can't live peacefully with each other and with everyone else, it's going to happen eventually. Leave Simon alone. Hell, leave everyone alone who doesn't want you around. We've already dealt with Alpha Carter and Beta Boyd. We won't have a problem dealing with you, too. The pride isn't subjugated the way it was before. We won't allow you to ruin the happiness we're working so hard to build."

Simon wasn't proud to say that he snuck out. He was angry, but he was grateful for Liam's presence and for his words. It was everything he'd been thinking, and everything he hadn't been able to say.

But he would, one day—possibly not when he was going on his first date with his mate, though.

Instead of going back to his office, he went to the rooms his family lived in. He'd told them he was going on a date tonight, and he'd wanted to avoid them breathing down his neck for more details. Luckily for him, all three of them were busy and didn't seem to be in. Unluckily for him, Jordan was spread out on his bed, reading a book.

He looked up when he heard Simon come in and rolled to his back. "You didn't tell me about your date. I had to hear it from Lisa. You wouldn't believe how happy she was to find out that me, your best friend, didn't know about it."

Simon sighed and closed the door. "I should have told you. I was busy."

Jordan sat up. "Too busy to talk to me?" he was keeping his voice light, but Simon could hear the pain in it.

He sat on the bed and reached for Jordan, cupping one of his ankles. "I'm sorry," he repeated. "I, well, I'm all over the place. You want to know something I didn't tell Lisa? In fact, no one but Val knows about this."

Jordan's eyes glittered. "Val?"

"Valentine. My date." Simon sucked in a breath. "Actually, my mate."

Jordan slapped a hand over his mouth. "Seriously?" he mumbled.

"Seriously. He's my mate, but I don't want anyone to know, not for a bit. And I need help. I've never been on a date, and I don't know what to wear."

Jordan looked Simon up and down. "All right. There's a lot of work to do, but we can do it. And while we do, you have to tell me *everything* about your Val."

His Val. Simon liked it.

Val looked at his reflection in the mirror. Tie or no tie? He wasn't sure. He didn't have anything planned for his first date with Simon. He'd wanted to plan, but every time he thought of something, he realized it was stupid and changed his mind. That meant that even though it was Saturday, he had no idea what they were going to do, and he knew that was a problem. It wasn't just because he didn't know what would happen tonight. It was also because now he didn't know what to wear.

He looked at his cat on the bed. "What do you think? Would a tie be too stuffy?"

Rain didn't answer. Not that Val had expected an answer, but it would have been nice to get one and have the decision taken off his hands. Instead, he had to make it.

He looked at himself again and dropped the tie on the dresser. "No tie. It's not me. Besides, it's too hot for a tie." And maybe, just maybe, he wanted Simon to have easy access to his throat.

He shook his head. He couldn't start thinking about them bonding, not right now. It was too soon, and he knew Simon would be uncomfortable with it. Val wouldn't even mention it, probably. Even though they hadn't actually spoken since the first time they'd met face to face, they'd texted every day, several times a day. Val liked Simon, at least what he knew of him, and Simon wasn't entirely comfortable with the date. It made sense after everything he'd told Val, and Val didn't know how to make him feel better.

The first thing to do would be to have their date in a place in which there wouldn't be too many people, Val thought. That way, Simon could relax and be himself. Where could they find such a place, though? Usually, Val went to the pub. There were a lot of people there, but it was familiar and comfortable. It wouldn't be for Simon, though. No, the number of people in there, especially on a Saturday evening, would be through the roof, and it would make Simon nervous, so that was out. What was *in*, though? Saturday was one of the worst days to have a date, especially when it came to the number of people running around town. Besides, with Simon being part of the Green Hill pride, everyone would be staring. They were curious, and while Val didn't blame them, since he was curious himself, he wished he and Simon could have some privacy. And maybe they would. He didn't know, and he probably should have more faith in his fellow Green Hill inhabitants.

He took a step back and looked at his reflection. He was wearing jeans and a nice dress shirt, and he'd left the collar open. He looked okay, he supposed, and he hoped Simon would share that opinion.

He was nervous. It didn't matter that he and Simon were mates. He still wanted to woo Simon. A lot of people would have taken it easy since they were mates, but that wasn't Val. Simon deserved to have a real date and to be seduced, especially after everything he'd gone through. Val was just the man to do that, but being mates made things both easier and harder.

Val already knew they would fit together perfectly, so he didn't have to worry about that. It carried expectations, though. Yes, they might be perfect for each other, but that meant that when he fucked up — and he would — it would be spectacular, and not in a good way.

He swallowed. He had to think of this date like any first date. Even though he and Simon were mates, Simon deserved that, and the bond didn't mean they would fall in love anyway. They might fit together in a way they wouldn't have if they hadn't been mates, but they could still fuck things up so much that they wouldn't want to be together.

That was the last thing Val wanted.

He moved toward the bed, rubbed the top of Rain's head, then smiled when he purred and rolled to his back, exposing his stomach. "I'm not falling for that." Val knew better. He took his hand away, ignoring his cat's glare. "If I touch your stomach, you're going to latch onto my hand, and I don't want to get to my first date with Simon all bloody. You're going to have to wait until later tonight."

Because Val was coming home tonight. It was way too soon for him and Simon to spend the night together, no matter how much he might want it. He didn't know if Simon did, and he wasn't going to ask. He wanted to take things slow. This was his last first date, the last time he'd share any firsts with anyone. If things went the way they should, he and Simon would eventually bond, and that would be for life.

Val couldn't wait.

He knew a lot of people were wary when it came to bonding with a shifter. It was like marriage, except there was no divorce. If he and Simon bonded, they would be bonded for the rest of their lives. Val didn't see it as a problem. He knew enough bonded people to realize they were blissfully happy. They fought, just like every other couple, but he wanted that happiness. He wanted to share his life with someone, and that someone was Simon.

On the one hand, Val was grateful that Fate, whoever she or they were, had taken the decision out of his hands. On the other hand, it made him nervous. He wanted everything to be perfect, just the way their bond would be, but life wasn't perfect, and *he* certainly wasn't.

He shook himself. "I should probably go before I start freaking out," he told Rain. "I'll see you later. Be good, and don't pee on my bed."

He headed out, grabbing his keys, his phone, and his wallet from the small table in the entrance. Before exiting the house, he looked around.

This was his home. He'd bought it a while ago, and he'd been working on fixing it in the way he wanted. It was his dream home, the place he'd always thought he would spend the rest of his life in. He might not now, though.

As far as he knew, all Green Hill pride members lived with the pride. There were other shifters in town, but they weren't part of the pride, and that meant that if things went the way they should with Simon, Val would probably have to move in with the pride.

He didn't know what to think about that.

As a human, he wasn't used to living with a lot of people. Even when he'd lived at home, he'd shared the space with only his family. The pride was different. Dozens of people lived under the same roof, and Val didn't understand how they made it work. He also didn't want to leave his house behind. He'd put a lot of work into it, but it wasn't finished yet. He could easily imagine Simon living here with him, maybe their children, if they decided to have any, but he wasn't sure it would happen. The pride was everything Simon had always known, and it wouldn't be easy to convince him to leave it behind, even though moving away didn't mean he couldn't be part of the pride anymore.

Unless it did. Val didn't know the new alpha well enough to understand what he would do, or what he expected from his pride members. Simon was his personal assistant, too, and that made everything more complicated.

But Val wouldn't find an answer by standing here. He had to focus on what was happening tonight rather than on the distant future.

Tonight, he had a date with his mate. He wanted it to be perfect because it was what Simon deserved. Everything else, he could think about later — much later if he had anything to say about it.

When it was time for Val to pick Simon up, Simon stayed by his bedroom window. He wanted to see when Val arrived so he could get to the door first. The last thing he needed was for Kevin or Anne to open the door and blab to Val. Even though Liam had talked to them, Simon knew better than to think things with them were over and smoothed out. Kevin and Anne wouldn't allow anything to stop them, not even the alpha mate. They would get their revenge, whatever it was. Simon hoped it would only be bad-mouthing him to the rest of the pride, but he couldn't be sure, which was why he was on alert right now, staring at the road that led to pride territory.

That was why he saw the truck approaching. It was high off the ground, and Simon wondered if he would be able to climb into it gracefully. Knowing himself, he would probably fall on his face, and Val would have to pick him up.

Simon didn't care.

Val already knew he was goofy. He'd seen him fall to his knees and had heard him talk to himself. He knew how Simon was, and he hadn't seemed to care. Simon had to keep that in mind before he talked himself out of going on their date.

He jumped to his feet, ready to go. He'd been ready for at least half an hour, and he was relieved he could finally head out.

Of course, things weren't that easy. He left his bedroom,

but he wasn't out of the set of rooms his family shared before his mother caught him. "Simon! You look gorgeous."

Simon almost rolled his eyes. He didn't, because he knew his mother meant it. "You *have* to think that. I'm your son."

"That doesn't mean I can't admit that you're a good-looking man. Being my son doesn't make you gorgeous. You do."

Simon couldn't help but smile softly. He wanted to rush out, but he didn't want to offend his mom. She'd always been there for him, and today wasn't any different. She was over the moon about the fact that Simon had a date, and even though he knew she wanted to, she hadn't asked for details, and she hadn't pushed to meet Val. She knew Val was human and that he probably would run away screaming if he were pushed into this too hard. No matter how accepting Val seemed to be, Simon didn't want to rush him into anything Val might not be ready for—or that *he* wasn't ready for. He wanted to tell his family that Val was his mate, but it was too soon.

Simon didn't know what he was ready for beyond this date.

His mother moved closer and messed with the open collar of Simon's shirt. "You're not wearing a tie," she said.

"You think I should have?" Simon had thought about it, but he'd gotten the feeling that Val wasn't a tie guy. He was more relaxed, and hopefully, their first date would be, too, but maybe Simon had gotten it wrong.

Simon's mom shook his head. "You need to be comfortable. If that's you without a tie, I don't think he'll mind."

"Thank you." He kissed her cheek. "But I have to go now."

She smiled, and Simon could see tears in her eyes. "Of course. Go. I can't believe you're going on your first date."

It would have been ridiculous coming from anyone else since Simon was already in his thirties, but the pride had been sheltered. They were finally breathing freely, and everyone was overwhelmed.

"Are you okay?" No matter how eager he was to get to Val, he couldn't leave his mom here crying."

She rubbed her eyes. "I am. This is just me being an idiot. You're an adult, not my baby boy, not anymore. Nothing will change that, and I have to accept it. I just want you to be happy."

Simon hugged her tightly, then, when she gently pushed him away, he headed downstairs.

He was late opening the door. Someone had already done it for him, and he looked down, horrified.

Gal was standing at the open front door, and he was talking to Val. Simon didn't know what to do. He didn't know what Gal would think about him and Val dating. He hadn't told Gal he and Val were mates, so Gal might think he had the right to forbid Simon to go anywhere with Val. It could be for whatever reason—because Val was human, and because he worked for the pride. Simon didn't know, and he wouldn't find out until he reached them.

He swallowed and went downstairs.

Val and Gal looked up at the same time. Simon couldn't have looked away from Val even if he'd wanted to—they were wearing pretty much the same thing, a shirt open at the collar and jeans, but Val wore them much better than Simon did. At least Simon wasn't overdressed or underdressed. It made Simon feel better.

Until he turned to face Gal. He held his breath, not knowing what to expect. He relaxed a bit when he saw Gal's soft smile. "I hope you don't need anything tonight," he said.

"I don't think I will. Go on your date. You deserve it, after all the hard work you've been doing for me."

"Are you sure? Because I can stay if you need me to."

Gal shook his head and reached for Simon, gently squeezing his shoulder. "It's Saturday night. I'm not going to work right now. I'm going to my mate, and you're going on a date. Have fun."

Simon nodded, a bit numb. He watched Gal walk away, then turned to Val. "You look dashing."

Val's eyes crinkled when he smiled.

Simon shouldn't have found it as adorable as he did.

"Dashing. I think I like that word."

"I hope you like a lot of words because Simon never stops talking," Kevin said.

Simon groaned. He tried to stop the sound so Kevin wouldn't know he was getting to him, but he couldn't, not right now.

He and Val both turned to the stairs. Simon had hoped they would manage to leave before anyone stuck their noses into what was happening, but he'd been wrong. Kevin was standing there, leaning against the railing, and it was obvious that he was trying to be seductive. He was biting his lower lip and batting his lashes as he stared at Val, making Simon's stomach churn unhappily.

He knew how Kevin was trying to get his revenge on him. He would try to seduce Val, and he would do everything he could to make that happen. He wanted to hurt Simon, and now he knew this was the best way to make that happen.

"I don't talk as much as Simon," Kevin continued. "Except in bed. Unless you want me to be silent there, too. I can be anything or anyone you want."

Simon turned to look at Val. They were going on their first date, and Simon knew Val didn't expect sex from him, not tonight. But now Kevin was offering himself up on a silver platter. Maybe that would appeal more to Val. Even though they were mates, it didn't mean he actually wanted to date Simon. He could have offered only because he wanted to get Simon in bed, and with Kevin, he wouldn't have to work hard to make that happen.

Val was gaping at Kevin, but as soon as Simon turned to face him, he shook his head and turned toward him. He offered him his hand, and Simon could only take it. "Ready?" he asked, ignoring Kevin. He might as well have been a fly on the wall.

Simon looked from Val to Kevin, who looked even angrier than he had in the kitchen earlier. He'd thought he was winning, but Val had dismissed him without a second glance.

Simon smiled. "Ready," he confirmed.

He and Val left the house together. Kevin was still on the stairs when the door closed behind them, but Simon didn't spare a thought for him. He couldn't, not right now, not during his first date with his mate. He and Val were the only people who mattered right now.

"What did you have in mind?" Simon asked once they were in the truck.

Val focused on driving away for a moment before answering. "Well, since this is our first date, I wanted to keep things simple. I didn't have anything in mind precisely, but I thought about it as I drove here, and I decided that dinner and a movie would be perfect, if you're okay with it."

Simon blinked.

Val had to force himself not to stare at him while he was driving. It was tempting, but he didn't want to crash the truck, not tonight of all nights.

"You didn't think about our date at all before tonight?"

"I tried, but I couldn't stop thinking about you. Honestly, I don't care what we do as long as I can do it with you and get to know you." Val was grateful that it was still light outside so he could see the blush on Simon's cheeks. Simon was always gorgeous, but especially so with his cheeks flushed.

"I thought about you a lot, too," Simon admitted.

"That's good." And it was. Val was relieved to find out that he wasn't the only one so obsessed. If Simon couldn't stop thinking about him, and he couldn't stop thinking about Simon, it meant they were on the right path.

"Dinner and a movie, then?" Simon asked.

Val hesitated. "I don't want you to be overwhelmed, so you can say no if you don't feel up to it, but I thought we could go to the pub I usually go to with my friends. It's one of my favorite spots in town, and the food is good."

"Why would I say no?"

"Because it's going to be busy. There are a lot of people there, especially on Friday and Saturday night. It's still early for the drinking crowd, but people like to eat there. It's not the perfect spot to have a first date, but I wanted to show it to you because I like it very much and spend quite a few evenings there. I know you're not used to being around a lot of people, though. We can choose another place if you're more comfortable."

Simon took his time answering, and Val liked that. Simon wasn't trying to please him just because they were mates. Val had wondered whether Simon would voice it if he didn't like his plans, and he was glad to see he would.

Except Simon shook his head. "I'm fine with the pub. I want to see this place you like so much. And if I'm too uncomfortable, we can still leave, right?"

"Of course. Besides, we'll be there only for dinner. Once we're done, we can go to the next town over and watch a movie."

"I'd like that."

They were silent for a moment, but it wasn't awkward. Val still found himself wanting to fill it, though. "Tell me about yourself."

"What do you want to know? There's not much to say. You already know that I've spent all my life with the pride. I wasn't allowed to leave, and it means that my life is pretty boring."

"I don't think anything about you can be boring. Tell me about your family."

Simon visibly relaxed, and Val smiled. This was what he wanted—for Simon to feel like he was with family when he was with him. It would take time, but this was a good first step in that direction.

"Well, with the way the pride is structured, I still live with my parents and my sister. It was the easiest way. Families tend to live together until the children get married, then they get their own rooms."

"Did you tell your parents about me?"

"I did. I told my sister, too. I didn't tell them you were my mate, though."

Val frowned. "Why not?"

"I guess I wanted to keep you to myself for a bit longer and not to rush into this. You're human, and I don't want their . . . enthusiasm to send you running. I already knew how my mother would react if I told her you were my mate. She already wants to meet you, and she thinks you're only my date. I can only imagine what would have happened if she'd known you were my mate."

"I look forward to meeting her." Val was surprised to find out that he really did. It had been a while since he'd last had a relationship, and even longer since he'd gone through the *meet the parents* thing, but it didn't scare him, not when it came to Simon.

"You'll meet them soon enough. I want things to go the right way between us, and that means that eventually I'll tell them about us."

"That's fine. You don't have to hide our relationship or be open about it. I'm not going to hide you, but you know your family and the pride, so you know how to deal with them better than I do." As long as he didn't keep Val a secret for too long, Val was fine with it. "Have you told anyone at all?"

"My best friend, Jordan. What about you?"

"Only my best friend, like you. I haven't told my parents yet because, like you, I wanted to get through this first date first. I think it's going pretty well, though."

Simon laughed. "It's only just started. There's still time to make a disaster out of it."

Val reached out, taking one of Simon's hands and quickly squeezing before returning his hand to the steering wheel. "Even if it's a disaster, it'll still be the perfect first date because I'm with you."

"You're a charmer, aren't you?"

"Not really. I just say whatever I think, and with you, it turns out I think a lot of sappy things. As long as you're charmed, though, I'm happy to continue."

"I'm charmed. Don't worry."

"You were telling me about your family." Val wanted to know everything there was to know about Simon. He wanted to be part of Simon's life, and that would only happen over time. In the meantime, though, he could start getting to know the people who were important to Simon.

"Well, there are my parents, Martha and Jim. Then there's my sister. She, along with Jordan, are my best friends."

"So they're going to be hard on me."

"I don't think so. As soon as I tell Lisa you're my mate, she'll welcome you, and Jordan was over the moon. I think they'd be happy even if you weren't my mate, to be honest. They want me to be happy, and now that we're free to leave the house and pride territory, they probably want the same thing I have."

"And what is that?"

"A job. A boyfriend or a mate. Someone outside the pride who can make them happy."

"Was Jordan ever your boyfriend?" Val wasn't jealous, but since all the pride members had been stuck in that house for God knew how long, he wouldn't be surprised if before becoming best friends, Simon and Jordan had been more.

"God, no. We tried kissing once when we were thirteen, but it was horrible."

Val laughed. "That's probably because you were thirteen, not because you were Simon and Jordan."

"I don't know. We never tried again, though. We decided we're better off as friends, and I don't regret that." He hesitated. "What about you? Do you have many ex-boyfriends?"

"None who still matter. The only person who matters in my life right now, at least when it comes to guys, is my best friend, Niall. We work together."

"Tell me about him."

Val did. Green Hill wasn't far from pride territory, and they spent the short drive talking.

They filled the entire date with talking. They talked over dinner at the pub and even attempted while they were at the movies. A few people had to shush them, and Simon giggled, burying his face against Val's neck.

Val wrapped an arm around his shoulders and held him close. He felt like he was in heaven. Their relationship was a budding one, but he already felt so close to Simon. They ended up holding hands through the movie, and the shy glances Simon gave him as they headed back to the truck almost brought Val to his knees.

He already knew what would happen when he drove Simon home. He could see that Simon was nervous again from the way he was playing with the bottom of his shirt. Val didn't say anything, though. He wanted Simon to feel comfortable enough to come to him when he was nervous, so he waited.

"What do you expect from me?" Simon finally asked when they were almost to pride territory.

"I'm not sure what you're talking about. What do you want to know?"

"Well, I know we're dating, but what's next? What do you expect from me?"

Val parked the truck in front of the house. The gates had been opened, so someone no doubt knew he and Simon were back. He turned the engine off, then twisted around in his seat to look at Simon. "What do *you* expect?"

Simon shook his head and unhooked his seatbelt before opening the door. "That's not fair. I asked that question first."

He was smiling, and Val smiled back. He hopped out of the truck to join Simon. "All right. I'll tell you what I'm thinking about doing."

Simon bit his lower lip and nodded. "I'm waiting."

"I want us to continue dating. I want us to have the kind of relationship everyone has. We date, get to know each other. Eventually, we sleep together. Then we move in together. We're going to bond, too. I want everything with you, Simon. Don't ever doubt that."

"Everything?" Simon asked.

Val nodded, then pulled Simon closer. He moved slowly, just in case, but he shouldn't have worried. Simon's eyes were wide, but he leaned against Val eagerly, tilting his head to look up at him. Val leaned down, unable to stop smiling as he kissed Simon for the first time.

This has been the perfect first date, and he couldn't wait to do it again. He already knew he would go home now that the evening was over, but that was okay. Simon deserved for things to go slow. He deserved for Val to take his time seducing him and making him see they could be perfect together.

Their first kiss was only the first step.

CHAPTER FOUR

It was time for Simon to talk to his family, as well as Gal and Liam. He and Val had been dating for several weeks, and everything was perfect. It was almost *too* perfect, and Simon was afraid that something would break. He could imagine it too easily, and it terrified him. Still, he couldn't keep Val a secret, especially not from his family and his alpha. He and Val were mates, and if things continued the way they were going, they would eventually bond.

He couldn't wait.

It might terrify him, but he wanted to spend the rest of his life with Val. They weren't there yet, but as long as he knew it was in the future, he could deal with it. He could deal with a lot, as long as Val was with him.

That meant telling his family and his alpha that he'd found his mate and that they'd been dating for a while without telling them. His parents would be disappointed he hadn't confided in them, even though they probably would understand.

Gal was different. Simon didn't know him well enough to be able to guess his reaction, and that petrified him. Simon's family wouldn't go anywhere. They would be there for him always, whether or not he'd disappointed them. He wasn't sure about Gal, though.

He didn't think Gal would kick him out of the pride merely because he hadn't told him about Val. Besides, Gal knew Val. He wasn't aware that Simon and Val were mates, but he did know they were dating. Hell, he'd talked to Val several times when he'd come to pick up Simon. Simon hoped that would be enough for Gal to accept this.

"You're going to have to leave this bedroom eventually."

Simon turned to look at Jordan. At least Simon wasn't alone. Val had suggested being present when Simon talked to his friends and family, but Simon hadn't wanted him to. He didn't know how they would react. If Simon got kicked out of the pride, he would have somewhere to go. Val had made that clear. If he wasn't, well, there would be time for Val to come around and meet his family and friends.

"Really. You *are* going to have to leave this bedroom," Jordan repeated.

He was sitting cross-legged on Simon's bed, and he'd been there for a while. Simon had told him that today was the day, and he knew that at least, he would always have Jordan. "I'm nervous," he admitted.

"What are you nervous about?"

Jordan already knew, but it wouldn't be a bad thing for Simon to talk it through. "That my parents will be disappointed that I didn't tell them. That they won't like the fact that Val is human. That Gal is going to get angry that I didn't tell him sooner. That he might kick my ass out of the pride."

Jordan snorted. "He's not going to do that. Come on. You've been working with him for weeks. Does he really act like the kind of man who would do something like that?"

Simon rolled his shoulders, trying to force himself to relax. "He doesn't," he admitted. Gal truly was the perfect boss, and Simon should have more faith in him.

"There. Besides, even if he gets angry, and I don't think he will, Liam will be there. He'll understand why you didn't want to tell people. He and Gal kept their bond a secret in the beginning, and their situation was even worse, because Gal was the new alpha. They won't kick you out. They might tease you, but they'll understand."

Simon hoped Jordan was right. "All right. Let's go."

Jordan scrambled to get off the bed. Since they were in Simon's room, his family was nearby, so he might as well start with them. That way, he could wait another day or two if he wasn't up to talking to Gal once it was over.

Simon couldn't remember a time in which he'd been happier. He was still somewhat wary, but he knew that was because he'd never had a relationship, and Val being his mate made everything more high stakes. If something went wrong, Simon stood to lose a lot. He would lose his only chance at having a mate and that kind of relationship, and of course, he didn't want that to happen. He hoped it wouldn't. While he and Val had been dating, it was only that for now. They hadn't bonded, and they hadn't had sex yet. Simon suspected Val wouldn't say no if he suggested it, but he was scared.

Everything was so new. He'd never had sex that involved feelings, and when it came to Val, that was what it would be.

Simon couldn't get out of the situation. When he got to the living room, his parents were there, as was his sister. She was curled on the couch scrolling through her phone, while his parents were watching TV. They all looked up when they heard him, and Simon swallowed.

He could do this. He had to.

"Jordan. I didn't know you were here," Simon's mom said. She got to her feet to hug Jordan.

Jordan's mother had died when he was a baby, and Simon's mom had been like a surrogate mom for him. Simon wasn't jealous. He wanted his best friend to have all the love in the world, and his mom was a loving person.

"Simon has something to tell you," Jordan said.

Simon glared at him. "You really had to open that big mouth of yours?"

"Sorry, not sorry. I just don't want you to chicken out."

"I won't chicken out. I just need to find the right words and to wrap my mind around it."

"You've had time to wrap your mind around it. Now you're just wasting time, and you know it. Come on. Tell them before I do it for you." His voice softened. "They'll be happy for you."

Simon turned to face his family. They were looking at him curiously, but he knew none of them would push. They'll wait for him to be ready to say whatever he had to say, and his heart swelled with love for them.

Jordan was right. Whatever happened with Gal and Liam, Simon would always have his family. He would always have Jordan, and now, Val.

He was still nervous, though. He swallowed—his mouth dry. "Okay. Well, Jordan is right. I do have something to tell you."

"Then you should tell us," Simon's father said. He sounded amused, but also slightly worried.

That was the last thing Simon wanted. He didn't want his parents to wonder what was going on. He wanted them to know that he was okay.

He cleared his throat. It was the hardest thing he'd ever done, except maybe going to the job interview with Gal, Liam, and Ellery. "I already told you about Val," he started.

Lisa snorted. "He's your boyfriend. So?" She sucked in a breath. "Are you moving in with him? Are you getting married?"

Simon shook his head. "We haven't been together that long."

"So? When it's right, it's right."

She couldn't have been more right. "When it's right, it's right," Simon agreed. "And in Val's case, it's right because he's my mate."

Simon looked around, waiting for his family to say something. His heart was racing, and he prayed that whatever happened next, he wasn't about to lose them.

"I still can't believe he's your freaking mate," Niall said.

Val barely looked at him. He was staring at his parents' house, wondering how they would react to the news he was about to dump on them. So far, the only person he'd told about Simon was Niall. He was also the only one Val had told that Simon was his mate, or rather, that Val was Simon's mate. He and Simon had wanted some time to wrap their mind around everything and to start to get to know each other.

And everything was going perfectly.

Val couldn't have dreamed for a better man in his life than Simon. Simon was adorable and sweet. He was everything Val could have ever wanted, and Val wasn't about to let him go. He wanted them to be together for the long run.

That meant he had to tell his parents about him.

He knew they wouldn't be happy about the age difference. Simon was twenty-eight, and he looked like he was in his early to mid-twenties. Val, on the other hand, was thirty-six. His parents were aware of the fact that shifters didn't age as quickly as humans, but they wouldn't care about that. Simon looked too young for Val, and Val wouldn't blame them for being wary.

He hoped they would accept Simon, though. Val loved his parents. He didn't have any siblings, so they were all he had, and he was all they had. He could easily imagine what would happen if they fought over this, and he wouldn't let that happen. His parents would eventually accept Simon. How long it would take was anyone's guess, but Val wouldn't give up his mate, not even for his parents.

"You look like you're about to get into a fight," Niall pointed out.

Val didn't think he was grateful for his best friend's presence anymore. "That's because I am."

"Why? They want you to be happy."

"You know they won't like the age difference."

"Simon's a shifter. Who cares about the age difference? As far as I know, he's fifty and you're the younger one."

"He's not. I'm actually older than him."

"Okay, so maybe your parents *will* have a problem with that. It's not a huge problem, though. Again, he's a shifter. He's going to look the way he looks now for decades. You're going to, too, if you bond with him." Niall grimaced. "I am *not* looking forward to looking older than you."

Val laughed, and everything was easier after that. Niall's words made him realize that while his parents might disapprove of the relationship, they couldn't deny the fact that Simon being a shifter trumped everything. It didn't matter how old Val and Simon were. Val was Simon's mate, and that was the only important thing in the situation.

"Let's go," he said. The sooner he did this, the sooner he could go back to Simon.

Niall slapped Val's back. "Atta boy. You'll see. They'll be happy for you."

He was right. Val sat his parents in the living room and told them he was dating a shifter, and that he was that shifter's mate. Then, he waited while his parents stared at him. He didn't have to wait long, though, because his father got up from the couch and came over to hug him. "I'm happy for you," he said.

Val relaxed and hugged his father back. "Thank you. I'm happy, too. Simon is everything I could have wanted, and more."

"As long as he makes you happy, I have nothing against him." He leaned back. "But I have a few questions."

"I expected you to. I'm listening."

Once Val's father was back on the couch, Val's mother reached for Val and squeezed his hand. "I'm happy for you, too. But like your father said, I have some doubts. I don't care that your Simon is a shifter, but I'm a bit wary of the fact that he's part of the Green Hill pack. We don't know anything about them. They stayed away from the town, and I can't help but wonder why."

It made sense. They'd always known about the pride, but with the way the pride had kept to itself, it was obvious that people were curious and thought there might be something bad happening. "I've been working at the pride for weeks. I can tell you that nothing bad is going on there. The only reason the pride stayed away from the town was their old alpha. He didn't want them to mingle, and they had to obey. He's gone now, though. He was replaced, and the new alpha is a great guy." Not that Val and Gal were friends, but they'd spoken several times about the house, mostly, but also about Simon and Liam. Gal didn't know Simon and Val were mates, but Val didn't think he would care.

"It *is* true that we've been seeing more pride members around town lately," Val's father said.

"The new alpha is a good one," Niall added. "We've talked to him, and we've been working there. They're good people. A bit weird sometimes, and of course, there are bad apples like everywhere, but Simon's a good man."

Val's mom looked at him. She was smiling, but her eyes looked suspiciously damp. "Then I'm happy for you. I don't have anything to say against Simon."

"But?" Val asked because there was always a but with his mom.

"But nothing. I'm a bit hesitant about the fact that you're his mate, but that's mostly because bonding with a shifter is much more serious than marriage. If you get married to someone, you can always divorce them. The same doesn't go for a bond with a shifter."

"We haven't been talking about that yet," Val assured her.

"But eventually, you will. You're his mate, and he'll want to bond."

"I want to bond, too. He might be the shifter between the two of us, but I'm ready for it, too."

"Once you do it, there's no coming back," Val's father warned.

Val should probably have been offended about the fact that they seemed to expect his relationship with Simon to go badly, but he wasn't. He understood that they were talking that way only because they were worried about him and that something would happen to him. "There is no telling whether a normal human-human relationship will go well or not. Every relationship is fragile in the beginning. There's no way to know what the future will hold, but I want Simon in my life."

"Of course, you can't tell how a relationship would go, but again, if you marry a human, you can get divorced. You won't be able to do that with your Simon."

"Maybe not, but I still have an advantage. If we decide to part ways, eventually, I'll be able to stop feeling guilty about the bond and leaving him." Simon, on the other hand, would have a harder time. Humans dealt easier with losing a mate, for whatever reason.

But Val wasn't planning on ever leaving Simon. He understood why his parents were afraid, but he wasn't. He wanted Simon. He was half in love with him already, and it wouldn't take much for him to fall in love with him entirely. When that happened, his and Simon's life would be twined together forever, and he couldn't wait. "I'd like to introduce him to you eventually," he said.

His mom finally smiled. "I can't wait to meet him. I was waiting for you to fall in love, and I can't believe it happened."

Val couldn't believe it had happened, either, but once he'd met Simon, there hadn't been a way out of it. Simon was just that lovable, and Val couldn't wait to begin their life together. He knew Simon was doing the same thing as he was right now, talking to his family, explaining what was going on between them. That meant that sooner rather than later, their families would meet, and while the thought was daunting, it was yet another step toward a future together.

They were getting there, and while Val didn't want to rush, he also couldn't wait.

Things with Simon's parents had gone well, and so had things with Val's. They'd texted as soon as they were done, and Simon felt better.

Val had told him that his parents had reservations, but that they wouldn't do anything about it. They were worried, and Simon got why. He was a shifter, and his parents were over the moon about the fact that he'd found his mate, but Val was human. It was normal that his parents were wary, especially with the way the Green Hill pride had kept itself separate from the town for so long. He hoped that eventually they would get to know him and come to like him, but even if it never happened, he knew he wouldn't lose Val. He would *never* lose him, not if Val had anything to say about it, and he did.

Simon was relieved that Val had asked if they could see each other today. He'd wanted to climb into his mate's lap as soon as he was done talking to his family, and that hadn't changed. He still had to tell Gal and Liam about him and Val being mates, but it could wait, at least for a few days. If Simon's parents hadn't cared, they wouldn't care, either.

Or at least, Simon thought so.

But Jordan was right. Gal was a good person, and he wouldn't care. If anything, he would be happy for Simon. They worked well together, and as far as Simon was concerned, they were becoming more than coworkers. He couldn't say they were best friends or anything like that, but they were friendly, and he knew Gal would want him to be happy, not just because he was his personal assistant, but also because he was his alpha.

Gal hadn't been wrong when he'd said that the two roles might make it harder for him and Simon to work together, but mostly, it was easy. Sometimes, it was hard to remember and to understand whether Gal was talking to him as his boss or his alpha, but things are working out, and Simon was positive about it.

And now, talking to Gal was the only thing left to do. Another day, though. Right now, Simon was waiting for Val, and since he couldn't find it in himself to sit on his bed, he bounded down the stairs. He might as well stay in the entrance, or maybe even stand outside on the porch. Val wouldn't mind, and he wouldn't tease Simon. Hell, he was probably just as eager to see Simon as Simon was to see him.

Simon was starting to relax when it came to Val. In the beginning, he'd been afraid to open himself up too much. He'd been afraid that Val would change his mind, that he wouldn't want to deal with him. It was hard to find a balance, especially when Simon had never had this kind of relationship before. Even if he took the mate thing out of the equation, he'd never had a relationship. He had a few flings with other pride members, but that was exactly what they'd been—flings.

Val was different. Simon couldn't stop thinking about him as he walked down the stairs, which was why he was distracted. If he hadn't been, he would have noticed Anne and Kevin sooner, and he could have turned around and gone back upstairs.

Instead, they noticed him, and they stood there, waiting for him at the bottom of the stairs.

Simon didn't know what they'd been doing, but he could

tell by their expressions that this encounter wouldn't be pleasurable, although since nothing was when it came to them, it wasn't surprising. He still forced himself to smile. He might not be the alpha or the beta, but he was the alpha's personal assistant, which meant that he was high in pride hierarchy, certainly higher than them.

"Anne, Kevin. How are you doing today?"

Kevin snorted loudly. "What do you care?"

"I wouldn't have asked if I didn't want to know."

"That's bullshit, and you know it. Shouldn't you be at work right now? I mean, you stole my job. The least you can do is to do it well."

"I have no problem doing my job." It was going to take Kevin a while to stop thinking about this situation as Simon stealing his job. Maybe he would never be able to do that.

Simon didn't care. He and Kevin had never been friends, and they never would be. He doubted Kevin had any friend apart from Anne. How those two had become friends was anyone's guess. They were both snakes, and they didn't trust anyone. Simon wasn't even sure they trusted each other, but he supposed that spending time together was better than always being alone.

"Look at how he's dressed," Anne said, looking Simon up and down. "You think he has another date?"

Kevin shrugged. "Maybe, but it's not going to last for long. I mean, can you imagine that hunk of a guy wanting to spend the rest of his life with him? Impossible."

Simon swallowed. He couldn't snap, no matter how much he wanted to. It wouldn't help. "Keep Val out of this conversation."

Kevin shook his head. "I don't get it. I mean, why should he want to be with you when he could be with me? Or maybe I just wasn't clear enough. Do you think he understood that I wanted to suck his dick that day?"

Simon knew his cheeks were flushed, and there was nothing he could do about it. He bit his lower lip, wondering how to answer and whether to answer at all. "Val doesn't want you. He wants me."

"And that's what doesn't make sense. Why should he want you? I'm sure I'm better than you at giving blow jobs, or in bed in general. I'm not even sure you've ever had sex. I wouldn't be surprised if you were a virgin. But either way, he's going to realize how awful you are, and he's going to dump you. Don't get too attached. It won't last long."

For the first time in his life, Simon wanted to hit someone. He wanted to punch Kevin, to kick his ass, to watch him bleed. It wasn't the kind of person he was, though, and it horrified him to feel that way.

He knew he should tell Gal about this. Gal had been clear when he'd told Simon that if anyone had anything to say about his position as his personal assistant, he wanted to know. He'd also told the entire pride, including Kevin and Anne, that he wouldn't tolerate bullying.

That was precisely what Kevin was doing right now, though.

Simon wanted to run to Gal and tell him, but he didn't want to be a tattletale. He might hate Kevin, but he suspected that a big part of what had made him a target was Kevin's resentment over not getting the personal assistant job. It would fade away—hopefully.

Simon shook his head and reached for the front door. Since he couldn't wait in the entrance, he would wait for Val outside on the porch.

"You're running," Kevin said, and he sounded victorious. "You know I'm right. And when he dumps you, I'll be there to pick up the pieces. I'll show him what being with a real man is like."

Simon froze, his hand on the handle. He didn't turn to look

at Kevin because he was afraid of how he'd react if he did. "You'll never have him."

"Keep telling yourself that, sunshine. I'll make sure to let you know once your boyfriend and I are an item. To be honest, I don't want a relationship. I just want to fuck him, and you'll know I gave him something you couldn't—a good damn time in bed. He'll beg for more, and you'll have to watch."

Kevin wouldn't be as pretty if he had his teeth knocked out, and it was tempting to turn around to do just that. Instead, Simon shook his head and opened the door.

He breathed easier once he was outside on the porch, but he could hear Kevin and Anne were still in the entrance, talking. He didn't want to know what they were telling each other. He didn't want to hear Kevin making plans with Val. Val wouldn't dump Simon. They were mates, and they would never lose each other.

Kevin didn't know that. Simon wasn't about to tell him that he and Val were mates. He didn't want to give him more ammunition.

Knowing he wouldn't lose Val, especially to Kevin of all people, made Simon feel better. Kevin had been trying to get a rise out of him, and he'd almost succeeded. Simon had managed to keep himself under control, though. Now that he had some time to think about it, he could see what Kevin had been doing. If Simon had hit him, he would have gone to Gal, no doubt crying. He would have told him that Simon wasn't a good personal assistant since he was going around hitting pride members, and that Gal should choose someone who was better suited, like him.

But it hadn't happened, and as Val's truck came up the driveway, Simon smiled.

His life might not be perfect by any means, but it was better with Val by his side.

Val could see something was wrong as soon as saw Simon waiting for him on the porch. He didn't know what it was, since Simon had told him that everything went well with his family, but he hoped he could help. Maybe Simon had decided to talk to his alpha after all, and Gal wasn't happy about what Simon and Val being mates would mean for the pride. Maybe it was something else. Val didn't know, but he was going to find out.

He parked the truck, and Simon walked down the porch steps. He rushed toward Val, and Val barely had the time to open his arms before Simon was between them. He hugged Simon close to his chest. Then he waited. If Simon wanted to talk, he would. When he didn't, Val hesitated. He didn't want to push, but it was obvious that Simon was in turmoil, and Val wouldn't be able to help if he didn't know what was going on. "I thought your family had taken it well," he said.

Simon leaned back so they could look at each other. "They did. They're happy."

"What is it, then? Have you told your alpha? Is that what the problem is?"

Simon shook his head. "I haven't told him yet, but I don't think he'll care. He found his mate, too, and he and Liam didn't tell anyone for a bit."

"Who hurt you, then?"

Simon hesitated, and Val tried not to take it personally. Even though he and Simon had been dating for a while now, he hadn't spent much time with the pride. He didn't know the dynamics between the pride members, and he wasn't looking forward to moving in with them considering how many of them there were all stuffed in one house. Still, if that was what made Simon happy, he wouldn't hesitate. He wanted to know what was going on first, though.

"Why don't we go somewhere?" he asked.

"I'm not up for a date, I don't think," Simon answered.

"Then we don't have to make it a date. We can go somewhere, stay in the truck, and talk. It's obvious you don't want to stick around here, and even though you haven't told me why, I want to give that to you."

Simon thought about it for a moment, then nodded. "All right. Let's go."

Val thought about what might be happening in Simon's life the entire time he drove. He didn't have a precise destination in mind, but he wasn't surprised when he found himself in the forest. He'd always loved hiking, and he'd driven them to one of his favorite spots. He parked the truck where he usually left it, but this time he didn't climb out. Instead, he turned the engine off and waited.

He could hear Simon breathing next to him, and he wanted to reach out. He didn't want to freak Simon out, though. He felt like it would be too easy to do right now, and he would never forgive himself for that.

Simon finally sighed. "It's not my parents or my family. They were all happy for me, and they can't wait to meet you. I had to tell my mom that you'll probably need some time since you're human, and she's agreed to wait."

"I can meet them tomorrow, if that's what you want. I don't mind."

Simon shook his head. "We should talk about it more. They're not a problem, though. I promise."

"And you told me it wasn't your alpha. Who is it, then?"

Simon bit his lower lip.

Val didn't like that he apparently felt he couldn't confide in him, but he tried not to take it personally. Whatever was happening, it probably had been happening long before Val came into Simon's life. They were still trying to fit their lives together, and Val had to remember that. Simon had had a life before him, and it would take some time to get to know all of it.

"You remember the man who was in the entrance when you picked me up for our first date?" Simon finally asked.

It took Val a moment to remember the guy. "I'm going to guess you're not talking about Gal, even though he opened the door, so the rude one, maybe?"

"Kevin is always rude. But yes, him."

"I hadn't thought about him since that day. Hell, even that day, I didn't think about him much. What's going on with him?"

"He's a bully. He and his best friend are, and I hate him. I was waiting for you when he and Anne confronted me. He's angry because he feels that I stole his job. He's the one who applied along with me."

"You didn't steal his job, though. Your alpha chose the one he preferred, and it was you."

"I've told Kevin that several times, but he doesn't believe me. He thinks that I did something, maybe slept with Gal. I didn't," he rushed to add.

Val reached out to take one of his hands. He linked their fingers together, then brought Simon's hand to his mouth, kissing the back of it. "I know you didn't do anything with your alpha. I trust you, and I don't care what someone I don't even know thinks. Besides, you and I didn't even know each other when you got the job, and I'm not stupid enough to think you've never had a lover. I don't like the thought of you with another man, but I won't get angry. Kevin has been using that against you, though, hasn't he?"

"He's been nasty every time I see him. He doesn't respect me, and I don't care if he does. I just want him to leave me alone. Gal chose me because he thought I would work better, and I agree. It would have been a disaster if Kevin had been given any kind of authority. But now he's taking things too far. He's not only teasing me about the job, he's teasing me about you, and I don't know what to do." Simon sucked in a breath and rubbed his forehead. "I don't even recognize myself. He said things, and I got so angry that I wanted to hit him." He dropped his hand and turned to look at Val. "I've never hit anyone. I don't want to start now. I don't want to hit Kevin, even though he deserves it. It scares me."

"You want to tell me what he said?" Val was already angry, and he doubted that knowing Kevin's exact words would help, but he felt he needed to know anyway.

Simon shrugged and looked away. "What you can expect from a bully? That I suck in my job, and that you'll leave me as soon as you realize you can have better. I don't know. It's Kevin."

"Does he know I'm your mate?"

"He doesn't. I didn't want to give him more ammunition."

Val wanted to hit Kevin, too, even though he hadn't spoken to him. He hated that someone was hurting his mate this way. He hated that they were trying to push Simon's self-esteem to the ground. He didn't want them to spend any length of time with Simon, but he knew he couldn't intervene.

This wasn't his battle, even though he would be more than happy to take it on for Simon. But he didn't know the pride. He didn't know the pride's dynamics, and he didn't want to make a mistake. Having the pride accept him, welcome him as Simon's mate, was the most important thing right now. It might not happen if Val started hitting people, even if they deserved it.

He reached out, pulling Simon closer and kissing his forehead. "I know there's not much I can do, but I want you to know that you can come to me with anything, even with this. I'll listen to you and won't judge. I don't know Kevin, but I don't like him. I can kick his ass if you want me to."

Simon chuckled before burying his face against Val's neck.

"As much as I want to accept your offer, I doubt it would be a good idea."

"Is there anything else I can do for you?"

"No. I'll have to face him eventually. I should tell Gal about it, though. He was clear the last time something happened with Kevin that he needed to stop being a bully, and he hasn't. Neither has Anne, although in this situation, she's not as involved. But they know Gal is against what they're doing, and he won't be happy. He also won't be happy about the fact that I hid it from him for so long." He tilted his head and kissed Val's neck. "I don't want to talk about them anymore, though."

Val held his breath. "What do you want to talk about, then?"

"I don't want to talk at all."

That was more than fine with Val. He wrapped his arms around Simon and pulled him closer, then kissed him. Simon opened his mouth eagerly, and Val delved in. They kissed for a while, but it wasn't enough. Val would never have enough of Simon. He wanted him always, in every second of his life, and he knew that would never change. Simone was his, and he was Simon's, forever.

Val dragged a hand down Simon's back until he reached his ass. He cupped it, holding his breath. He and Simon should probably talk about this before they did anything, but he didn't want to break the moment. He wanted to chase the memories of Kevin from Simon's mind, at least for a bit. If sex was what it took, he would be more than happy to provide Simon that, even though the truck wasn't exactly comfortable.

Instead of pushing Val away, Simon groaned and turned toward him.

Val's eyes widened when Simon climbed into his lap. Simon didn't hesitate, though. He settled onto Val's lap, reached for Val's jeans, and opened them.

Val sucked on his lower lip, hoping Simon wanted the same thing he did. He grabbed the waist of Simon's jeans and followed it with his fingers until he found the button. Then, he hesitated, but Simon would have none of that.

He cupped Val's face with both his hands and kissed him. Val took that as a go-ahead, and he opened Simon's jeans, taking his cock out of his underwear and wrapping his fingers around it. Simon whined and tried to press closer, but the truck being what it was, there was no space for him to move. Simon couldn't be comfortable with his head tilted forward and his neck crooked, but he didn't protest, and Val continued stroking his cock.

Val wiggled, trying to settle in a better position. He wanted to make Simon come, to feel him pulse in his hand. From the way Simon moaned and panted, there was a good chance he'd manage, and soon. He didn't want Simon to come alone, though, so he was relieved when Simon finally touched him, too.

"You have big hands," Simon whispered.

Val almost laughed. "I do."

"Can you wrap it around both our cocks?"

Val looked down. Neither of them was exceptionally endowed, something for which he was grateful right now. "Probably."

Simon huffed and undulated his hips. "Then what are you waiting for? A written invitation?"

Val laughed and obeyed. He liked that Simon asked for what he wanted, and he was eager to deliver. Just like Simon had asked, he let go of Simon's cock to wrap his hand around both their dicks. It was a tight fit, but that made it even better. Their cocks rubbed against each other, sending Val straight to heaven and making pleasure coil in his groin. Simon moved on top of Val, thrusting against him and clutching his shoulders so he wouldn't topple to the side. Val couldn't wait to do this in a bed, with lube on hand and more time, but right now, it was perfect. He and Simon were perfect together.

Simon came first, shooting all over Val's t-shirt. Val should have thought of that, but he couldn't seem to think about anything right now, not if it was beyond pleasure. So he focused on that, stroking Simon through his orgasm and pushing himself closer to his at the same time. Simon had just slumped against Val and was lightly biting his neck when Val came, too. He didn't know if it was because of Simon's presence on top of him, Simon's teeth on his neck, or their mingled scents in the truck , and he didn't care. He screwed his eyes shut and gritted his teeth.

Simon snuggled against Val once it was over. He looked like he wasn't planning on moving anytime soon, and Val wasn't about to protest. He held his mate close and closed his eyes, smiling.

"I guess that was one way to make me feel better," Simon said.

"Happy to help when I can."

"You did. Thank you."

It was probably too soon to tell Simon this, but Val would be there for him every time he needed him, for the rest of his life.

Chapter Five

Now that Simon had told his family, it was time to tell Liam and Gal that he and Val were mates, as well as what had been happening with Kevin.

Simon wasn't looking forward to it.

He didn't want to create problems for anyone, not even Kevin. He understood why Kevin was acting the way he was, at least in part. He would have been angry, too, if he hadn't gotten the job. He would have been disappointed, but he would never have lashed out the way Kevin had. That was all on Kevin, and Simon was done tiptoeing inside his own house. He was done checking himself for the way he acted. He didn't want to stick mostly to his rooms just in case Kevin was around the corner.

He sighed. He was angry at Kevin, but he also wished he didn't have to do this.

"What's going on?" Liam asked.

He, Simon, and Gal were having lunch in Gal's office. They did this when they were overwhelmed with work, but Simon was relieved. He hadn't been about to explain to Gal what had been happening in front of everyone else at lunch, and the thought of asking to talk to him made Simon's stomach churn. He wanted to explain in a relaxed setting, and lunch in the office was what he'd been thinking about. It was so hard to get the words out, though.

"Nothing's been happening," he said.

He should have known he wouldn't be able to fool Liam. Not only had they known each other since they were babies, but Liam was a good alpha mate. Since Gal had arrived and Liam had taken over the charge, he'd honed his instincts when it came to the pride members. It was scary how easily he could read some of them, and especially scary that Simon was one of them.

Liam stared at him, one brow arched, until Simon sighed and put down his sandwich. "Fine. There are two things I wanted to talk to you about." He looked at Gal. "To the two of you."

Gal frowned and looked down at his salad. "I'm not going to like this, am I?"

"Parts of it, I hope you will. The other part, though, no. You won't."

Gal sighed. "Fine. Start with the good news."

"I can wait, if you'd rather eat lunch first." Now Simon felt guilty about interrupting the meal.

"Come on. You know we barely have time to eat, let alone have a conversation. Just get it all out. We're listening."

Simon swallowed. He looked down at his sandwich, then back up at his alpha and alpha mate. "You know I've been dating Val."

Liam smiled. "We do. Things have been going well with him? Is he one of the things you wanted to talk to us about?"

"Yes. We've been dating, but there's more to it. He's actually my mate." Simon waited. He didn't know what he was waiting for—an explosion of anger, a smile. He had no idea how this would go.

He should have had more faith in his alpha, though, because the only thing Gal did was smile and say, "Congratulations. I understand why you didn't tell us before, and I'm not angry. That was the good news, right?"

Simon's shoulders slumped in relief. "It was."

Liam elbowed Gal in the ribs. "Of course it's good news. What did you think?" He turned to look at Simon, narrowing his eyes. "You thought we wouldn't be happy for you."

Simon was ashamed that he'd thought that now. He should have known better. "I didn't know how you would react. I'm sorry I didn't have faith in you."

Liam opened his mouth, but Gal shook his head and took one of his hands. "Think about it. We didn't tell anyone we were mates in the beginning."

"That was because you were the new alpha," Liam said. "It would have looked bad if you'd just arrived and found your mate."

"You know that's not the only reason. Yes, it was a big part of it, but I also wanted to keep you to myself for a bit. And I did. See how things are going now? We barely have time to see each other."

Liam grimaced and leaned against Gal's side. "Fine. And I'm not angry." He looked at Simon. "I'm a bit disappointed you didn't think you could trust me with this, but I do understand. Even though we grew up here, we weren't friends." He hesitated. "I'd like for that to change. I like you, Simon. I like how you've been taking care of my mate."

Simon's cheeks heated. "I haven't been doing anything."

"We both know that's not true." Liam took a drink of his glass of water, then straightened his shoulders. "All right. We heard the good news. I think it's time for the bad news. I suspect I know what you're going to say, and Gal is right. He won't like it."

Gal grunted. "Am I the last one to know what's going on here?"

Liam gestured at Simon to go on.

There was nothing Simon wanted less, but he knew there was no way out. "It has to do with Kevin and Anne. Well, mostly Kevin. He hasn't stopped harassing me since I got the job instead of him."

Gal's frown grew deeper. "What do you mean by harassing

you?"

"Just that. Every time he sees me, he has something to say about how I stole his job, including insinuating that you and I, well, you know. That I gave you something in exchange for the job. Now that he knows I'm dating Val, it's gotten even worse. He's been going around telling me and anyone who will listen that eventually, Val will dump me for him. He tells people what he and Val are going to do in bed, things like that. He's a bully." There was nothing else to say. Gal knew what kind of person Kevin was, and he'd already warned him to check his mouth. Kevin hadn't, not when it came to Simon anyway.

Gal grimaced and leaned back in his chair. "Has anyone heard him say those things? You keep saying that he says that to you and anyone who will listen, but I thought he was smarter than that."

"He's also angry. I'm sure that a few times, there was no one around, but he hasn't been careful. He doesn't know Val is my mate, either. I think he believes that he can push me into breaking up with Val."

"And he doesn't know it's not going to happen," Gal said. He rubbed his face, then reached for his cell phone on his desk. "I'm calling Forest. Even though I'm the alpha, this is his kind of thing. He'll know what to do, hopefully."

Simon wasn't hungry anymore, and he pushed his sandwich away. He hadn't wanted to do this, mostly because he didn't want Kevin to be kicked out of the pride. He never wanted anyone to be kicked out. He could only imagine how hard life would be for someone who had lived here all their life and was suddenly without the pride, a home, a job, or anything else.

Still, Simon was relieved that Gal and Liam were happy for him and Val. He was happy that he was going to see Val soon. He was also starting to want to move away from the pride, even though he'd been born here and he loved the new pride.

He didn't know if that was possible. Every current single pride member lived in this house. None of them had ever moved out, but that had more to do with Alpha Carter than it did with Gal. Simon didn't know what Gal would think about it, but he knew that in other prides, packs, and shifter groups, some members lived away from the main house. It was a possibility he couldn't stop thinking about. He wanted to start a life with Val, but the pride house didn't feel like the right place to do that.

It was something he was going to have to talk about with Val before bringing it up with Gal, though. Besides, Simon had more than a few things to think about right now, and he had to focus on them first. Once it was done, though, he would have to talk to Val, and the thought made him nervous.

What if Val didn't want to move in with him? What if Gal said no to Simon moving away?

Val was early picking up Simon. He should probably have waited in the truck, just like he had every other time, but he was curious. He hadn't yet been invited inside the pride house as Simon's boyfriend or as his mate. He'd been inside only for work, so he knew what to expect, but it wasn't the same.

So he left his truck and headed to the house.

He knocked, looking around. He and the team had done a good job on the roof, and they'd started inside the house. They were almost done with the bathrooms, and next would come the kitchen. The house needed a lot of work, but Val could see how much some of the members loved it. They'd done their best to patch up the problems and fix it, and even though in some places they hadn't quite managed, it didn't matter. They'd made Val's job easier by trying to keep up with the repairs, and Val appreciated it.

A man he didn't know opened the door. He'd seen him before, and it wasn't the guy who was bullying Simon, so he relaxed. "Hi. I'm Val. I'm here to pick up Simon. I'm a bit early, so he probably doesn't know I'm here yet."

To Val's relief, the man smiled. "I'm Ellery. Please, come in. You can wait here in the entrance."

"Thank you." Val stepped in and looked around. It looked just like every other time he'd been here, and his brain immediately went to the small repairs and other things he could do in this room to make it even better.

"I'll go grab Simon, unless you want to call him?" Ellery said.

"He's probably busy getting ready, and I don't want to disturb him."

"He'll be eager to see you. I'll go tell him you're here."

"Thank you." Val didn't know how to behave when it came to pride members, and he didn't enjoy feeling awkward, but he was grateful for Ellery's offer.

That left him alone in the entrance, and he went back to looking around. That didn't last long, though, unfortunately. A door slammed in the distance, and two people stepped into the room. They were talking, their heads close together, but Val recognized them instantly. He almost growled, and he might have if he hadn't preferred *not* to attract attention. He hoped they would pass by him without noticing him, but of course, they didn't.

The man, Kevin, looked up. His eyes widened for a moment when he noticed Val standing there. Then, his lips curled into a wicked smile, and Val knew he wasn't going to like what was about to happen.

"Anne, why don't you head over to the kitchen? I'll be right there." Kevin said.

The woman looked from Val to Kevin and smiled. "Of

course. You know where to find me when you're done."

"I'll see you soon." He paused dramatically. "Or maybe not so soon."

He turned his attention to Val. Val was tense, and he waited to see what would happen. He was half tempted to slam Kevin against the wall and threaten him for hurting Simon, but he knew better. Even though he was Simon's mate, he was still a guest here at the pride, and he didn't want to do anything that would get him kicked out. He never wanted Simon to have to choose between his family and his home, and him.

"Why, hello. I didn't expect you to be standing there when I came in," Kevin said.

Val crossed his arms over his chest. "Why should you have expected me?"

"Unfortunately, you're not here to see me, are you?"

"I'm here to see Simon," Val confirmed. He realized it probably had been a stupid thing to say when Kevin's smile widened.

He moved closer, swishing his hips. He was clearly trying to be seductive, but he was working too hard at it. Even if Val didn't have Simon in his life, he wouldn't have fallen for it.

Kevin stopped when he was so close to Val that his chest brushed against Val's arms. He put a hand on Val's bicep and squeezed. "Well, I understand why Simon is with you. What I *don't* understand is why you're with Simon. What does he give you that you can't get with someone else?"

"None of your business."

"Oh, I was just wondering. Simon and I are friends."

Val snorted and dropped his arms to the side. "No, you're not."

Kevin's expression twisted for a second. Then, he smiled again, but it was more forced. "What has he been saying about me? They're all lies."

"I'm pretty sure they're not."

"Well, you don't know Simon as well as I do. I've been living with him all my life. I know the kind of person he is. He's a liar. That's how he got the job, you know? It was supposed to be mine, but he fucked the alpha."

Val was both horrified and curious to see where Kevin was going with this. "I don't believe that."

"That's because he's good at acting innocent. Has he offered you his ass yet? Is that why you're with him? Because I'm better than him in bed."

"Don't talk about him that way." Val wasn't sure whether Kevin was trying to convince him to sleep with him or to make him jealous, and he didn't like that he *was* jealous at the thought of Simon with someone else. Val wasn't the jealous type, though, not even when it came to his mate. Simon had been an adult before he met Val, and Val knew he hadn't been celibate all that time. He didn't want him to have been, either. Simon's past was what had made Simon who he was, and the man Val loved.

Kevin's gaze flickered to a spot behind Val's body, but before Val could turn around to see what was happening, Kevin pushed himself into his space and threw his arms around Val's neck. Val jerked back, but he couldn't move back, not with the way Kevin was hanging on to him.

Then Kevin kissed him.

Val froze for just a second. If it had been anyone else, he would have gently pushed him away and told him that he didn't want him that way. Instead, he unhooked Kevin's arms from his neck, still not kissing him back, and pushed him so hard that Kevin's back hit the wall. Kevin was laughing, though. That didn't make sense unless Kevin had done this for a specific reason.

Val looked behind himself.

Simon was standing there on the stairs, staring. Val didn't

know how much he'd caught of the conversation or what he'd seen, but from his horrified facial expression, Val could tell that he'd seen the kiss. He wasn't alone, either. Ellery was there, and he had a hand on Simon's shoulder.

Simon shook his head. He turned around and ran up the stairs before Val could say anything.

"Simon!" Val cried out. He moved toward the stairs, ignoring Kevin, who looked like the cat that ate the canary. Val paused when he reached Ellery. He didn't know if he was welcome here, and even though he wanted nothing more than to go after Simon, he didn't want to do something that would get him kicked out of the house.

To his relief, Ellery smiled at him. "Follow him. I'll contact Gal and Liam and tell them what's happening." His focus moved to Kevin. "They need to know anyway." He told Val where to find Simon's room, and Val didn't wait for him to say anything else. He rushed up the stairs, hoping he wasn't too late, and that Simon would listen to him.

The only thing Simon could feel was pain. Well, there was a bit of confusion too, and anger, but he couldn't get the image of Kevin and Val kissing out of his head. He didn't know if he'd ever be able to.

He'd been over the moon when Ellery had come to tell him that Val had already arrived and was waiting in the entrance. He hadn't even thought about what it would mean. He'd just finished getting ready and headed to Val, eager to go on their date. Ellery had teased him about how happy he was, and Simon hadn't stopped smiling.

At least until he'd seen Kevin throw his arms around Val's neck and kiss him.

Simon knew what he'd seen, but he couldn't believe that Val would do something like that. It had to have been Kevin, which wasn't surprising after everything Kevin had done, but Simon still couldn't stop thinking about it.

He was only half relieved when someone knocked on the door. His mom or sister had probably noticed him come running back into their rooms and wanted to talk to him. They were no doubt worried, and there was nothing Simon wanted less than to talk to them or anyone else right now. Still, he knew they would keep hammering on his door until he opened. That was just the kind of people they were, and if they were worried, they wouldn't let anything come between them and Simon.

He briefly looked at himself in the mirror, trying to school his expression. He couldn't do anything to hide the pain in his eyes, but he hoped they wouldn't look at him too closely.

Then, he plastered a smile on his face and opened the door.

It wasn't his mother or sister. It wasn't his father, either. It was Val, and he was panting as if he'd run through the house to get to Simon. Knowing him, he probably had, and Simon stood there, staring at him.

Val raised his hands. "We need to talk," he said. "Please, don't slam the door in my face."

Simon's first instinct was to tell him to leave, but he knew Val deserved the opportunity to give him an explanation. If things had gone the way Simon thought and Kevin had done everything by himself, it would be cruel to push Val away because of Simon's insecurities. Yes, he'd been expecting something like this to happen since Val and he had started dating, but he'd been doing his best to push those thoughts away. That internal voice sounded like Kevin, and it pushed him to believe that he wasn't good enough.

He knew he was, though. He was Val's mate, and he loved him. Those were the only things he was sure about right now, and he wasn't about to push Val away. That would make Kevin happy, and it would mean he had won, and Simon didn't want that to happen.

He stepped to the side. "Come in."

Val blinked at him. He was clearly surprised that Simon wasn't about to slam the door in his face. He stepped into the bedroom, cautious, and looked around. Simon closed the door, then leaned against it.

He couldn't look at Val. Every time he did, a flash of an image of Val and Kevin kissing invaded his mind. "Who opened the door for you?" he asked.

Val turned his attention back to Simon. "Ellery told me where to find you, and I think your sister opened the door. She didn't realize something bad was happening. She smirked when she saw me and told me where your room is. I'm pretty sure she thinks we'll be having sex or something."

Simon grimaced. Lisa was going to tease him endlessly about this, at least until she found out what had actually happened. "Can we not talk about sex and my sister in the same sentence?"

"Of course." Val stood there, in the middle of the room. "I guess we need to talk about what just happened."

Simon sighed. "Sit down."

"Where?"

"Wherever you want. You can take the bed if you want. I don't think I can sit down right now." Simon had nervous energy to burn, so he started pacing the room, even though it wasn't big enough for that to relieve the stress.

"I didn't want to kiss him. I promise you that. I've never wanted anyone the way I want you, and I would do nothing to put what we have in jeopardy," Val said.

Simon stopped in front of him and shook his head. "I know it wasn't your fault. You don't have to apologize."

Val frowned. "Are you sure? Because you ran away from me before I could say anything downstairs."

"I didn't want to give Kevin the satisfaction of seeing how

I reacted to what he did. I know why he did it. He saw me on the stairs, and he decided he might as well take the opportunity."

"I suspect you're right. He looked behind me before kissing me. I should have tried harder to push him away, though."

"You couldn't have. I saw what happened. I would be surprised if his head hadn't hit the wall." Of course, it hadn't been enough to stop him from laughing. He'd found this exhilarating, which told Simon just how mean he was.

"I hate that you had to see that."

Simon's heart softened just a bit. He knew this wasn't Val's fault, and he didn't want to hold it against him. He wasn't sure he would ever be able to get the image out of his mind, though.

"What can I do to make things easier for you?" Val asked. He got to his feet. "I can go if you want some time on your own."

"Stay. Please." Simon might not want to have to think about what had just happened anymore, but he also couldn't allow Val to leave him. He needed him, now more than any other time.

Val nodded. "Tell me what I can do. Please."

"Nothing. You've already apologized, even though you shouldn't have. I know this was all Kevin. I don't want you to worry about whether or not I will break up with you. I won't."

Val moved closer and gently took one of Simon's hands. "There's something else, though."

Damn him for having learned to read Simon so easily in such a short time. "Nothing you're involved with. But Kevin has been bullying me and others for years. He's been constantly pushing us down, telling us we're not good enough, and he wasn't the only one. Alpha Carter and Beta Boyd did the same thing. A lot of us believe it now. I did for a long time."

"But you don't anymore?"

Simon shrugged. "Not really. I mean, I got a job I never thought I would have, and I know that I wasn't good enough to get it. I still got it, and I worked hard to learn. I'm good at it now."

"Of course you are."

Simon looked Val in the eyes. "And there's you. You're my mate, which means I have to have done something good in my life. You were destined to be with me, and we were destined to meet when we did. I won't allow Kevin to ruin everything. I can't. This is what he wants, and he won't win." Not this time, not ever again if Simon had anything to say about it.

"Is there anything I can do at all?" Val asked. He looked worried and eager, and that was enough to tell Simon how much he cared.

It would be hard not to think about Val and Kevin kissing, but Simon knew he would have to, and that he could. It was the only way for him and Val to go forward instead of backward. He didn't want to lose Val, and he didn't want to lose his job. He wouldn't give Kevin anything.

"We should probably talk to Gal and Forest," he said.

"I'm sure you're right. They need to know."

"They do. I've already told them what Kevin and Anne have been up to lately, and they were angry. They wanted to talk to the two of them on their own, though, which was why they haven't done it yet."

"Will they now?"

"They will." Because they cared about the pride. They weren't born here, and they hadn't grown up here, yet they seemed to care more than Kevin. They wanted the pride members to be happy and settled, while Kevin only wanted to sow chaos.

For the first time ever, Simon was glad that Kevin would be kicked out of the pride. Hell, he found himself hoping he would. He didn't like it, but this was what Kevin was transforming him into, and he wasn't going to fight it, not on this.

For a few horrible movements, Val had thought he'd lost everything. When he'd been climbing the stairs and trying to find Simon's room, he'd thought this was the last time he would have the opportunity of talking to his mate. He wanted to strangle Kevin for it, and he was blaming himself. Surely he could have done more. He could have pushed Kevin away sooner. He could have made it obvious that he didn't want Kevin.

Now, he knew he shouldn't have berated himself. Simon knew what had happened, and he wasn't angry. Well, he wasn't angry with Val. He was obviously pissed at Kevin, and Val shared that opinion. As far as he was concerned, he hoped Gal kicked the guy out of the pride. He knew that sometimes shifters did things like that, and he could imagine how much it hurt to lose everything you'd ever had, including your family and your home.

But right now, he didn't want to talk about Kevin. Kevin was a bully, and he'd been doing this for years. It was time to start ignoring him and putting it behind them.

Val reached for Simon, half wondering if Simon would step away. He didn't. Instead, he allowed Val to pull him into his arms.

"I thought I'd lost you," Val murmured against his mate's head. He kissed his hair, inhaling his scent. Something settled deep inside him, and he knew that if he and Simon could get over this, they could get over anything. There was no way Val would allow anything like this to happen again. If he had to stay out of the pride house to make sure it didn't, then he would.

That might make it complicated to move in with Simon, but they hadn't talked about it yet, so he didn't want to assume he would. He'd never been in Simon's place, but he could imagine how hard it was to forget what he'd seen.

Val had had nothing to do with the kiss, but Simon had still seen it. Kevin had made sure Simon would, and he'd succeeded. Only in part, though. He'd probably meant to have Val and Simon break up, but they weren't going to. They would weather the storm, and they would come out of it stronger, and still together.

Simon settled against Val's chest. "I know we should go find Gal and tell him, but I don't want to. I don't want to leave you right now."

"I'll come with you." Simon could try to leave Val here, but there was no way Val was letting him out of his sight, not right now.

"Is it bad that I want a moment with you? Alone?"

"Of course not. I always want a moment alone with you, and we've just been through something terrible. I'm sorry you had to see that."

Simon pushed away from Val and glared at him. "Stop saying that. I know it wasn't your fault."

"It doesn't change the fact that you saw it."

Simon grimaced. "Okay, so you're not wrong. I'm pretty sure I won't be able to forget the image anytime soon. But you know what? Every time it pops up in my mind, I'll think about you. I'll think about how I know you, and that I'm sure you wouldn't do something like that on purpose. I'll think about when you kiss me, and it's like heaven. I don't want to lose that. I don't want to lose you or to allow Kevin to win. I won't let him do that. He might have tried to break us up, but it won't work."

Val hesitated. He'd been thinking about this for a while

now, but he hadn't brought it up yet. He wasn't sure now was the perfect moment to do it, but he couldn't think of a better one. "We could bond," he said.

Simon snapped his mouth shut and stared at him, so much that Val thought he'd made a mistake. It was too soon for them to bond. They'd been dating for several weeks, but it wasn't long enough. But Val was falling in love with Simon, and he knew nothing would change that. He wasn't going anywhere, not until Simon told him he didn't want him anymore, and he prayed that would never happen.

He didn't want to lose Simon, and he wanted them to be even closer. If Simon had been human, Val would probably be proposing to him right now. Instead, Val wanted to bond.

"I'm in love with you," he added. He wanted Simon to say yes. "I know what I want, and what I want is you, forever. I don't ever want to have to leave you here at night after one of our dates. I want to go to bed next to you and wake up with a smile on my face because I know that the first thing I'll see when I open my eyes is you. I want us to share a life, a home. I know it's soon, but I don't think it matters. We can wait if you're not ready for it. As long as I have you, I'll be happy. But I want you to feel secure in our relationship, and obviously, you don't, not entirely. I don't know if it was Kevin's fault, but if there's anything I can do to show you that I'm not going anywhere, then I want to do it."

It was more than that, though. Yes, Val wanted Simon to be sure he wasn't going anywhere, but he also wanted to put his mark on Simon. He knew it wouldn't be the same thing. He couldn't bite Simon, so the spot on Simon's neck in which Val would eventually drink his blood wouldn't be obvious to anyone. Still, people would know. He would be able to claim Simon as his own. He would have everything he wanted with Simon—a bonded relationship, a home, a life, a family.

That would only happen if Simon was okay with it. He still

hadn't said anything, and Val wasn't sure how to take it.

"I want to do it," Simon finally said.

Val's legs felt like jelly, and he sat down on the bed. "You mean you want to bond with me?" he asked because he needed to be a hundred percent sure that was what Simon was saying.

"I do. I've been thinking about it again and again, but I never said anything because I thought it would freak you out. You're human. I thought it would be too soon for me to suggest something like that. I know humans usually take things much slower."

Val shook his head. "Does it really matter that I'm human? I want you, Simon. You're the only thing I want. Besides, I want us to bond, too. I want us to be one for the rest of our lives."

Simon stared at Val for a moment longer, then, to Val's surprise, reached for his t-shirt. "Then, you have me. I want us to bond, too." He pulled his shirt off and dropped it.

Val lost himself in staring. Simon was gorgeous. He'd always been gorgeous, even with clothes on, but there was something about his naked body that appealed to Val particularly. Simon was vulnerable, yet strong. He looked like he knew what he wanted, but there was also a hint of hesitancy in the way he moved as he took off his jeans.

Then he stood naked in front of Val, and Val couldn't think about anything anymore. The only thing he could focus on was Simon and what was about to happen, and he opened his arms.

Simon laughed and stepped closer.

Val had a hard time believing they really were doing this, but they were, and he'd never wanted anything more. He wrapped his arms around Simon and pulled him close, and together, they fell onto the mattress.

It was slightly more complicated for Val to get rid of his

clothes, since he was spread out on the bed with Simon on top of him, but together, they managed.

Simon's cheeks were flushed when he reached for his nightstand, taking lube out of the drawer. Val didn't say anything about it. He didn't want Simon to be ashamed of what they were about to do, or to think he should be. They were in love, and they were doing what anyone else in love did–becoming one.

"How do we do this?" Val asked because that was one thing they needed to know.

"I don't know. Every time I've had sex before, I was the bottom. I guess it's because I'm smaller and everything."

"But you want to fuck me right now?"

Simon looked away, his cheeks red. "Not if you don't want that."

"Of course I do."

Simon's eyes went wide. "Are you sure? Because I don't expect you to do anything you don't want to do."

"I have nothing against being fucked." While it might not be what Val preferred, he didn't expect Simon to do anything he wasn't ready to do himself.

Simon nodded. "All right. I want to fuck you, then."

Val couldn't think about a more perfect way for them to bond than with Simon inside of him. Still, he was tense, especially after Simon started stretching him. He knew what to expect, of course. He'd been on Simon's end many times. He'd been fucked, too, although he hadn't loved it. He didn't know if that would change now that he was with Simon, but he would do everything he could to make Simon feel comfortable. If Simon sometimes wanted to fuck him, then he would be more than happy to make that happen. He was pretty sure he would love everything with Simon. Simon was careful, preparing Val as if he were precious. He obviously wanted Val to feel no pain, and that was more than what Val could say about the other guys that he'd let do this. Even if he didn't love it, he knew he wouldn't be as against it as he had been until now.

Val was writhing by the time Simon decided it was time. He'd driven Val half-crazy by sucking his cock as he prepped him, and Val felt like he was about to explode.

That was until Simon pushed inside him. Then, the only thing he could think about was the pain. He knew it would pass, but this was always the worst part of being fucked. Some days, he wasn't sure why anyone did it.

Then, Simon kissed him, softly, gently, murmuring that he had to relax, that he would stop if Val wanted him to.

Val found that he didn't. They were about to bond, and he wanted that to happen with Simon inside of him. He wanted them to be one while they did it, and he tilted his head to the side to give Simon easy access.

"Still sure?" Simon asked.

"More than ever."

That hurt, too, but only for a second. Then Simon started sucking the blood that pooled out of the wound he'd just created, and pleasure invaded Val's groin. For a second, he'd thought he'd come, and then he realized he hadn't. He looked around, wondering how he was supposed to drink Simon's blood. Simon seemed to understand what he was looking for, and without moving away from Val's neck, he reached up and sliced his own neck with a nail that looked suspiciously like a claw.

Val didn't pause to ask questions. Instead, he latched onto the wound and drank.

It was blood, so it didn't taste good, but if it meant that he and Simon would be bonded forever after this was over, Val would do it eagerly. He drank, wondering how much he should suck down, how their relationship would change once they were bonded. He wasn't even sure he would feel anything.

Then, he felt it.

Something snapped into place. It was like having a second consciousness in his mind. He recognized it as Simon, and he wanted to reach for it. Simon came forward, and they twined together, once separated, now one. They fed off each other's feelings — pleasure, love, satisfaction — until Simon went rigid against Val. Val could tell what had happened without looking down. He could *feel* it. Simon had just come, and it was almost as if Val had, too.

He tore his mouth away from Simon's neck and tried to breathe. Simon was still moving inside him, still pushing him toward the edge, demanding Val come. Val bit his lower lip so he wouldn't cry out and screwed his eyes shut when he let go.

Simon had filled him, both with his release and his blood, and Val had welcomed him. Nothing would ever separate them now. Simon would always know what Val felt — which would be a challenge until they both got used to it. But Val had never backed down in front of challenges, and this was one he was eager to face.

CHAPTER SIX

Now that he and Val were bonded, Simon wanted them to stay in their small bubble in his bedroom. They were still wrapped around each other, but he knew it wouldn't last forever. It couldn't, not when he still needed to talk to Gal and Liam. He had to tell them about his and Valentine's bonding, but also about Kevin.

Ellery had stood up to Kevin, and Simon should do the same. Gal wouldn't be happy that Simon hadn't told him how bad the situation with Kevin was. He'd been clear when he'd hired Simon that he wanted Simon to be honest with him. Simon understood why. Gal and Forest were still trying to learn how to deal best with the pride, to settle in as alpha and beta, and to be accepted. They needed to guide the pride with a strong hand, though, and people like Kevin were undermining their authority. If they allowed bullying to happen, why should the pride trust them?

Simon would never forgive himself if what he'd done — or rather, hadn't done — meant that Gal wasn't respected as alpha anymore. He hoped it wouldn't happen, but to make sure it didn't, he had to speak up. No one else had, but then, he'd been the main target of Kevin's hate lately.

"You're thinking hard," Val said, stroking a hand down Simon's still naked back.

Simon shivered. It was tempting to stay right where he was, but he couldn't. Maybe later, once he'd done everything he should be doing.

He propped himself up on his elbow and looked down at

his mate. "I was thinking about Kevin."

Val grimaced. "I have to say I didn't expect you to mention another guy while we were in bed together naked."

Simon couldn't help but smile. "You know what I mean. I have to talk to Gal. I have to tell him what just happened."

Val sighed. "I think he already knows, but do you want me to come with you?"

Simon liked that Val hadn't assumed he would be coming with him. Simon wanted him to, but he knew better. This was a problem *he* had to face, and besides, he was the pride member, not Val. He suspected Gal would want to talk to Val, too, but that could come later. And he had no doubt that Gal already knew — he had ears and eyes everywhere in the house.

"I think I should talk to him alone first."

Val nodded. He clearly wasn't happy, but Simon knew he wouldn't push. He could feel the anxiousness coming through their bond, the worry, but also the love and trust.

He didn't know why he'd thought that Val didn't love him. He hadn't, not really, except for a few seconds when he'd seen Val and Kevin kiss. He'd allowed those few seconds to freak him out, but luckily for both of them, it hadn't lasted long. He didn't want to lose Val, and now, he wouldn't.

"Am I allowed to move around the house?" Val asked.

"What did you have in mind?"

"I'm kind of hungry. We were supposed to go out to eat, but since our plans changed, I should probably find some food. Unless you want me to leave? I can come back tomorrow."

"I'd like for you to spend the night here, if you can," Simon said. His heart raced at the thought of spending the night with Val, but he also couldn't imagine not being with him tonight, not after what they'd just shared.

"I'm not going anywhere until you kick me out. I'll head to the kitchen, then?"

"Sure. Just tell anyone who gives you trouble that you're with me."

Val arched a brow. "Are you saying that I should tell them that I'm your mate?"

Simon's cheeks heated, but he didn't look away. "Why not? Everyone will know soon enough anyway."

Val reached up and fingered the bite mark on his neck. "I have to say, I'm tempted to go around without my shirt so everyone can see this."

"Please don't. I don't want you to start a riot. But yes, feel free to tell people you're with me and that I told you it wasn't a problem for you to stick around."

"I guess it's going to make it easier for me when I move in."

Simon frowned. "Move in?"

"Once we decide we're ready for it, of course."

"I think that bonding means you're ready for pretty much anything. We're as good as married. I'm not sure I understand what you meant about moving in, though."

Val looked uncomfortable, but he, too, faced it head-on. "I figured that since none of the pride members live in town, you wouldn't be allowed to. I don't even know if it's something you guys do. The only shifters I know who live in town aren't part of a group."

Simon bit his lower lip. "I don't know, either. None of us were allowed to leave the house when Alpha Carter was still around, but Gal is different. I'll have to talk to him."

"You think there's a chance he'll allow you to move in with me? No offense, because I love this house, but it's a bit too crowded for my taste."

Simon laughed and leaned down to kiss his mate. "Most of the time, it's a bit too crowded for my tastes, too. And yes, I do want to move in with you rather than the other way around. I'll ask Gal what he thinks about it."

"And if he says no? You're not just a pride member. You're

also his personal assistant."

"Then we'll figure something out when the time comes."
But Simon hoped Gal wouldn't have a reason to say no.

Gal wasn't a bad alpha, and he was considerate of what the
pride members wanted. So far, no one had asked to move out,
but Simon thought it was more because this was what they
were used to. None of the pride members had ever lived outside of the pride house in recent years. Simon was probably
the only one ready to do such a thing, and while being a trail-
blazer made him anxious, he was ready to do just that if it
meant a life with Val. He would even quit his job if it came to
that. Now that he knew he could have a job and be good at it,
he hoped he might find something in town if Gal put his foot
down.

Val's stomach growled, and he laughed. "I guess I should
go downstairs."

"I have to go downstairs, too. I doubt I'll find Gal in his
office, not at this hour. He might be in the living room,
though." Even though it would be easier for him and Liam to
watch TV in their room, Gal made a point to spend time in the
common areas of the house. He was the alpha, and the pride
was a family, albeit a huge one. They should spend time together that didn't include working.

Simon and Val quickly washed up and dressed. Simon
could still feel the echo of the moment in which Val had
sucked his blood in his neck, and he reached up, touching the
spot. He knew the wound had healed—it always did when
shifters mated—but it wouldn't disappear. It would always
be there, even if it was invisible to Simon and everyone else.

He and Val separated once they got downstairs. Val smiled
and squeezed Simon's hand, then headed to the kitchen while
Simon went to the living room, hoping to find Gal there.

He didn't. Unfortunately for him, Gal was nowhere to be
seen, while Anne and Kevin were sitting on the couch by the

window, talking. They both looked up when they heard him.

Kevin's smile was wicked and mean-looking as he got to his feet. He came closer, and Simon held his breath. He wanted to turn around and run away, but he knew he couldn't. He had to stand up to Kevin, and that was what he was going to do.

"Are you done crying, then?" Kevin asked.

At that moment, Simon realized that Kevin didn't know Val had stuck around. He didn't know that Simon and Val were mates and that they'd bonded. It was tempting to throw that in his face and see what happened, but Simon wanted to protect his relationship with Val. They might be bonded, but they hadn't been together long, and he didn't want Kevin to make it his life mission to destroy it.

"You know, he's not a bad kisser. I guess he was distracted, though. I'm sure that the next time we kiss, it will be even better," Kevin said.

Simon squeezed his hands into fists. He wouldn't hit Kevin, no matter how much he wanted to. He opened his mouth to tell Kevin to fuck off, but someone beat him to it.

"I didn't kiss you back."

Simon turned to see Val coming into the living room. He looked angry enough that he might hit Kevin, and Simon moved to his side, wrapping his arms around one of Val's. Val looked down at him, smiling softly, before turning his attention back to Kevin.

"You need to leave Simon and me alone."

Val couldn't remember a time in which he'd been so angry. He wasn't surprised at what he'd heard Kevin say, but he wished Simon hadn't had to listen to it.

Kevin's eyes were wide. "What is *that*?" he asked, staring at Val's neck.

Val didn't even try to hide the bite mark on his neck. He'd left the collar of his shirt open on purpose so people would see it. "It's the sign that Simon and I bonded."

"You're his *mate*?" Kevin sounded incredulous.

Val understood why. He'd been playing on the fact that he believed Val would dump Simon soon, but now, obviously, that wouldn't happen. It wouldn't have happened anyway, but Kevin didn't know that.

"We're mates, yes," Simon confirmed.

Kevin turned to him. "And you knew this entire time?"

"Of course I did. And you made yourself ridiculous by trying to seduce Val. I knew you were lying when you said the two of you kissed willingly. I still hate you for what you did."

"You ran away. When you saw us kissing, you ran. You thought he was kissing me, didn't you?"

Simon looked sad when he answered. "I didn't, no. I knew Val wouldn't do something like that to me. I won't deny it hurt and that I acted on instinct, but I know the truth."

Kevin crossed his arms over his chest. He was smiling, and Val knew it wouldn't be good. "So you don't trust him. You thought he was kissing me, and you ran away. Why on earth did you bond with him? Bonding won't stop him from cheating on you."

"That's enough," Gal snapped from behind Val.

Val jumped, then scrambled to let the alpha pass. He'd talked to him a few times, mostly about the jobs that still needed to be done around the house, but this was the first time he'd seen him in full alpha mode. He was terrifying, and Val was relieved he wasn't in Kevin's shoes.

Kevin had paled so much that he looked like he might be about to faint. "Alpha Brennan."

"What do you think you're doing, Kevin?" Gal asked.

Val didn't miss how Kevin called him Alpha Brennan rather than Gal, as if he hadn't been granted the privilege of calling the alpha by his given name.

"We were just playing around. We're friends."

Simon snorted loudly, loud enough that everyone turned to look at him. His cheeks flushed and he leaned closer to Val, who wrapped an arm around him. "We're not friends. We've never been friends, and with everything Kevin's been doing, we never will be."

Gal nodded and turned his attention back to Kevin. He wasn't alone. With him was a man Val had seen a few times around the house but had never talked to. He knew it was the beta, though, which meant that Kevin was about to get his ass handed to him.

"I want you in my office," Gal said. "Now, Kevin. Head there, and don't touch anything. I'll know if you do."

Kevin opened his mouth, then shut it. "What are you going to do to me?" he asked.

He sounded scared, and while Val felt sorry for him, he had to remember that Kevin had brought this on himself. If he'd left Simon alone, if he hadn't been a bully, he wouldn't be in danger of being kicked out of the pride.

Gal shook his head. "I don't know yet. We need to talk, though." He turned to look at Anne, who was still sitting down, her expression horrified. She snapped her mouth closed when she saw him looking at her and swallowed so heavily that even Val could hear her from where he was. "I want to talk to you, too. Come to my office in an hour. Don't be late."

"Of course, Alpha Brennan."

With that said, Gal turned around. He focused on Val and Simon, and Val wondered if he was about to get kicked out, too. Just like Kevin had noticed the bite on Val's neck, Gal did, too. His gaze went right there, and Val held his breath.

He released it when instead of snapping, Gal smiled. "Well, I guess I should say welcome to the pride," he told Val.

Val blinked. After what had just happened, he'd fully expected to be yelled at. "Thank you."

Gal sighed. "We'll talk later, all right?"

"We don't have to talk if you're busy. I understand, even though I'm human."

"Thank you for that, but I still want to talk to you and to welcome you to the pride properly. Besides, I think the three of us should talk together. Simon has to make some decisions right now, and so do you."

He was no doubt thinking about who was going to move where, and since Simon seemed to be okay with it, Val hoped Gal would allow them to move into Val's house. No matter how much this was home for Simon, it wasn't good for him to live here, as the situation with Kevin had shown. Gal and his beta were doing their best to deal with the pride, but they were only two men. They couldn't work miracles, and Val didn't want Simon to be exposed to this kind of meanness every day. Besides, he couldn't see himself living with so many people. It might be normal for shifters, but it wasn't for most humans, and he wanted his privacy.

Gal's beta stopped before following him. "Welcome to the pride from me, as well."

"I'm human," Val said. He hadn't stopped Gal when Gal had welcomed him into the pride, but he felt slightly more comfortable with the beta.

The man smiled at him and offered him his hand. "Forest. I've seen you around the house, working. I'm sorry I didn't introduce myself sooner, but as you can imagine, being the beta of this pride is hard work."

Val shook his hand. "I understand, and thank you. I'm Val."

Forest nodded and let go of Val's hand. "It doesn't matter that you're human. You're Simon's mate, and he's a pride member. That makes you one, too, because of who you are to him. It's not complicated, just a bit overwhelming."

He left, too, and Val and Simon were alone together in the living room. Anne had scampered away through another exit, and Val was relieved that he wouldn't have to deal with her, even though so far, she wasn't the one who'd given him and Simon the most trouble.

"I was wondering when this was going to happen," Liam said as he strode into the living room.

Val almost groaned. He'd wanted some time alone with Simon to make sure his mate was okay, but it didn't look like it was going to happen. Thankfully, Simon looked happy to see Liam.

"When what was going to happen?" he asked.

Liam smiled. "Both Kevin getting his ass kicked and you two bonding. Congratulations."

"Thank you."

"Bonding is truly fantastic, isn't it?"

Simon's cheeks were even redder now. "It is."

Liam's smile was understanding. "Why don't we get a snack in the kitchen? I'm sure you want to talk, and I doubt Gal will be done anytime soon, so I don't have anything else to do."

"He said he wanted to see us later."

"You can talk to him if you want, of course. Actually, you *should* talk to him. But I'm the alpha mate, and I can tell him what's going on if you'd rather wait. Considering what's going on, it wouldn't be a bad idea to give Gal time to relax. Besides, you're a new pride member. We should get to know each other."

Val sighed. He'd wanted time alone with Simon, but he supposed they would have it soon enough. If Simon thought that spending time with Liam was the right thing to do, then Val would go along with it. It wouldn't be a bad thing for him to get to know his new family.

Simon felt awkward, even though he knew he shouldn't. Liam wasn't just the alpha mate. He was a friend, even though they hadn't been close until recently. But he knew that whatever Liam had to say, it wasn't bad. He'd obviously been happy about Simon and Val bonding, and he'd been nothing but welcoming to Val. Besides, he wouldn't make any kind of decisions when it came to Simon and Val on his own. He was the alpha mate, and he could take Gal's place in a pinch if Gal was unavailable, but still. He would want to talk things through with his mate, and now, Simon understood why.

Talking with Val only seemed to make things better and clearer, and it made it even easier to make decisions, like the one about who would move into whose house. Simon knew that if he asked, he would be assigned another set of rooms so he could move away from his family and be with Val. He wouldn't do that, though. Hopefully, Gal would allow him to move out of the pride house entirely. He wasn't going far, just into town, but he needed freedom. No matter how much he loved the pride, after everything that had happened, he wanted some distance from it. He was surprised no one else had asked to move away, but he realized that maybe people were afraid Gal would get angry and forbid them to.

Simon was afraid, too, but he had a reason to take that step. He wouldn't let anything stop him, not even fear—not anymore.

"I'm really sorry about everything that happened with Kevin," Liam said as they put together a snack and drinks.

Val shrugged. "You have nothing to be sorry about. I don't know exactly how the pride works, but I can imagine it's a lot of work. You can't have eyes everywhere."

"You're right. We can't. We should be more careful, though. I know Kevin and Anne. I know what they do and how much damage they inflict. I should have done something about them a long time ago."

"You were focusing on other people," Simon intervened. He didn't want Liam to feel guilty or like he wasn't properly doing his job. "Besides, you're not the only one who knew they were up to something. You might feel like you should have done more, but I don't see what else you could have done. You and Gal told me to come to talk to the two of you if something more happened, and I didn't. I should have right from the beginning."

Liam leaned against the counter, peering at Simon. "Why didn't you? I mean, I can understand that you didn't want to talk to Gal or Forest. They're strangers, even though they're our alpha and beta. They haven't been here long, but I grew up here. I would have understood."

Simon hated the pain he could hear in Liam's voice, but he understood it. "I wanted to be your friend, but none of us is used to having friends. Besides, you're the alpha mate, and I was slightly intimidated. You weren't just Liam anymore, and that made it even harder to come to you to talk about this. There's also the fact that I thought it was trivial. Yes, Kevin is a bully, and he's been mean to me for what feels like forever, but he's never hurt me."

Liam wrinkled his nose. "I beg to disagree. You don't have to hit someone to hurt them. He hurt you, even if he did so with words."

Simon swallowed. That much was true. Kevin and Anne had been pushing him down, telling him he wasn't good enough. They'd been angry with him because he'd gotten the job as Gal's personal assistant, and they'd made him pay for it.

He didn't regret it, though. It hurt, yes, but it had also made him grow. He was a good personal assistant to the alpha, and now he had a mate. No matter what Anne and Kevin had been trying to do, things were looking good for Simon, and he couldn't find it in himself to resent them.

Well, not much anyway.

Jordan suddenly burst into the kitchen, looking around as if he expected someone to be beating Simon. His eyes widened when he saw Simon. He rushed toward him, wrapping his arms around him and almost making both of them fall. "I heard what happened. I'm sorry you had to see Val and Kevin kiss. Are you okay? What's going on with Kevin? People are saying that Gal is kicking him out of pride because he kissed your mate. Is it true?"

Simon laughed and patted Jordan's back. "Breathe. I can't answer any of those questions unless you let me get a word in."

Jordan moved back. He didn't go far, though, holding Simon at arm's length. "So? What happened? Did Val really kiss Kevin?"

"I didn't," Val said. He was standing next to Liam, and the two of them were looking at Simon and Jordan.

Jordan jumped away from Simon. "I'm sorry. I didn't mean anything with the hug. We're best friends, that's all."

Val chuckled and shook his head. "I didn't say anything about the hug. I'm not going to forbid you from hugging Simon. That's something Simon should decide. I didn't kiss Kevin, though. He kissed me, and he made sure to do it when he knew Simon would see us. But don't worry, we already worked things out, and we're good."

Jordan squeaked, and Simon knew he'd seen the mark on Val's neck. Val ought to button his shirt, although then Simon wouldn't be able to see so much skin.

Jordan turned to look at Simon. "Are you okay, then?" he asked instead of asking about the bonding, even though Simon was sure he was curious.

"I'm fine. I won't deny it hurt, but I always knew Val

wouldn't do something like that."

"I bet you're happy you bonded. When were you going to tell me?"

"When more than half an hour had passed? I was going to tell you soon, I promise. I wanted to tell Gal first, but then we stumbled onto Kevin and Anne, and everything went to hell from there."

Not anymore, though. Whatever happened to Kevin and Anne, it was out of Simon's hands, and he honestly didn't care. They'd brought it onto themselves, even though they'd had a warning. Gal had been clear when he'd told the entire pride that he wouldn't accept any kind of bullying from anyone. Ellery had been through a lot because of Kevin and Anne, and they were lucky they hadn't been kicked out then. They might not be as lucky now.

"I want details later," Jordan whispered.

Simon laughed. Yes, his life was looking up. He had a family, his pride, his best friend, and his mate. He still didn't know if he would be allowed to move out. But even if he wasn't, he knew he wasn't alone. He had a support system, and he would use it.

The four of them went to sit outside on the porch. Simon was flustered every time Val touched him, even though it was innocent touches, like making sure he was comfortable and that his glass was always full. Simon didn't think anyone had ever cared about him that much. His parents loved him, of course, but they'd had to be careful to keep the love confined to their rooms when Alpha Carter had been in power. It had been hard to be a family that way, but they'd managed, and now Simon was an adult. He was probably better adjusted than a lot of people in the pride, and he had to thank his parents for that.

This kind of attention was different from what they could give him, though. It was a mate's attention, a different kind of love, and Simon reveled in it.

Yes, Simon was planning on moving out of the pride house and start a life of his own. It was about time he did that. He hadn't been allowed to have a life when Alpha Carter had been the alpha, but he was positive that Gal was different. He and Val could start making plans, even though they should probably wait until they talked to Gal to settle down, but they could start.

They could dream.

Val had never thought he would feel at home with an entire pride of tiger shifters, but he did. He wasn't about to move in here, not if there was another solution and Simon could move in with him, but he couldn't deny that it wouldn't be such a bad thing if he had to move. It wouldn't be that much of a hardship, even though getting used to sharing a home with so many people wouldn't be easy. He was positive, though. Gal was doing the right thing with Kevin, and it was all that mattered. At least that way, if he and Simon had to stay here, Simon would be okay, and he wouldn't have to deal with Kevin again. Val could get used to anything as long as he had Simon and Simon was okay.

"I'm really sorry about what happened," Liam murmured after a while.

The four of them were sitting on the porch, darkness surrounding them. So far, they hadn't heard anything about Gal or Kevin, but then, Liam had warned them that it would be a while before Gal was done with Kevin. Val had no intention of seeing the alpha tonight anyway. Right now, the only thing he wanted to focus on was Simon. They could talk to Gal tomorrow or the day after that.

"You have nothing to be sorry about," he tried to reassure Liam. "You've been nothing but welcoming to me, even when you didn't know I was Simon's mate. Hell, you were welcoming even when I hadn't even met Simon yet. You're a good person, and the perfect alpha mate."

Liam snorted. "There's no such thing as perfect, but thank you." He bit his lower lip. "It's not easy, you know? Until recently, I was just a pride member. I never thought I'd have to do this. It wasn't even a possibility, not when Alpha Carter was still in charge."

"But you are, and you're doing a good job," Simon said. He was cuddled against Val's side as if he couldn't bear to move away from him. That was more than okay with Val since he couldn't bear to move away from Simon, either.

"I'm doing my best," Liam said.

Val thought his best was good enough, but then, he wasn't a shifter. He'd never lived with shifters. He trusted Simon when it came to this, though. If he was going to move in with the pride, he would have to trust Simon for a lot of things, which was good since they were bonded now. He would have trusted his mate even if they hadn't been, but he felt more settled in their relationship now.

"What's next for the two of you?" Jordan asked.

Val wasn't sure what to make of Simon's best friend, but he realized it was mostly because he didn't know the guy. He seemed nice enough, and he'd clearly been worried for Simon earlier. That meant he was all right in Val's book. Anyone who was worried for their best friend the way Jordan had been was a good person, and Simon wouldn't be friends with someone untrustworthy.

Simon tensed against Val. "I don't know. What are you asking exactly?"

Val could see the frown on Jordan's face, even in the darkness. "Well, I was wondering if Val was going to head home tonight."

Simon relaxed again. Val realized what he'd been tense

about. He still hadn't talked to Gal or anyone else about moving out of the pride house, and it made him nervous.

Val didn't understand that, but again, he wasn't a shifter. It was obvious that shifters were used to living in large groups, and he would never push for Simon to leave his home, not if Simon didn't want that. But Simon had told him he did, and Val couldn't wait to start a new life together. Besides, it wasn't like they were moving to another state. There were only going to town, where Val lived, and it would take Simon only ten minutes to get back to the pride house when he needed to.

"Well, this was supposed to be a date," Simon explained.

Jordan snorted. "What a date, huh?"

Val couldn't deny that. "It didn't go as planned, but I can't say I'm sorry."

"I bet you're not. You and Simon bonded."

That was something Val would never regret. "We did. I didn't expect the date to end like this, but I'm happy it did." He tightened his arm around Simon's shoulders, and Simon pressed himself harder against him. "As for what I'm going to do now, I'm hoping I can stay here for tonight. Of course, that only goes if Liam is okay with it." Simon had already agreed, but he wasn't the one in charge.

"You don't even have to ask," Liam said. "I might be alpha mate, but neither Gal nor I are going to police the pride members. Alpha Carter would have, but we're not him. If Simon wants to have you stay for the night, it's more than fine with us, and he doesn't have to ask for permission. He's an adult."

Val relaxed. That was a good way to look at the situation, and it gave him hope that Liam would look at the rest of it the same way. If Gal forbid Simon to move out, Liam might be a good ally to have. They weren't there yet, though.

"I want Val to stay the night," Simon murmured.

Val kissed his forehead. "I will." Because he had no

intention of staying away from his mate for another night. They'd only dated for a short time, but they were bonded, and to Val, it was as good as being married. He wouldn't expect to have to stay away from his husband overnight, and the same went for his mate. He didn't care what people thought, and he knew the law. He might not be a shifter, but he knew the council didn't allow anyone to intervene when it came to mates.

That was another reason why he hoped Simon would be allowed to move out of the pride house. Even if Gal couldn't stop Simon from doing that, he could make his life harder. He could kick him out of the pride or not allow him to come back. The pride was everything Simon had known until now, and his family was part of it. Val wasn't entirely sure which way Simon would go if he had to choose, although he hoped Simon would choose him. He would never demand that from him, though. He couldn't fully understand how Simon felt, but he did know that it would be an impossible decision to make.

He hoped it wouldn't come to that.

He didn't ask, though. Liam wasn't the one who made this kind of decision, and they would talk to Gal soon enough. He didn't want to worry until then. Instead, he wanted to focus on Simon and their bond.

The little group disbanded soon after. They heard several doors slam, and Val couldn't help but wonder if it was Kevin. Had Gal kicked him out of the pride? Was he already packing? Or had Gal allowed him to stay? Or maybe he'd kicked him out but had given him until morning to get his things together and find a new place to live. Val had no idea, and he didn't care. He didn't see why he should. Kevin had almost ruined everything, and he couldn't help but be angry at the man, especially after the way he'd talked to Simon earlier. Val would be disappointed if he had to see Kevin again, and he hoped he wouldn't.

He and Simon headed to Simon's room after they said goodbye to Liam and Jordan. Val was surprised to see that the living room they'd passed through earlier wasn't empty anymore, although he should probably have expected that, since Simon shared the rooms they were in with his parents and his sister.

The three of them looked up from the TV when they heard the door open, and while Simon's sister smiled wickedly, his parents stared at Val as if they'd seen a ghost.

Simon shuffled his feet, but he pulled Val inside and closed the door behind them. "Mom, Dad. This is Val. My mate." Simon's mother shot from her seat, but Simon held a hand up. "And before you realize that on your own, we just bonded. You can talk to us as much as you want tomorrow morning, but right now, we need some time alone. We had an evening that you wouldn't believe."

Simon's parents seemed to be respectful of the fact that both he and Val needed space, but Val still hugged Simon's mother and shook Simon's father's hand, and he accepted their congratulations.

Then, they were alone again in Simon's room, and Val pulled Simon against his chest.

"You think everything will be okay?" Simon asked. His voice was slightly shaky, and Val wished he could give him a positive answer.

"I don't know what's going to happen tomorrow, and I can't promise everything will be okay. I *can* promise I'm not going anywhere, though. I love you, Simon, and we're bonded. This is forever for me."

"It's forever for me, too."

"Then we'll find a way." They would have to, because Val wasn't giving Simon and their relationship up.

CHAPTER SEVEN

Everyone knew Val had stayed the night. It was the only explanation why every single pride member Val and Simon crossed path with stared at them.

Well, it was either that or they'd heard about Kevin.

Simon still didn't know what had happened to Kevin. He didn't want to care about it, but he found that he couldn't stop thinking about him. Had Gal kicked him out? Simon should be happy, but to his own surprise, he wasn't. He didn't want Kevin to continue torturing him, but he also didn't want him to find himself completely alone in the world, even though that was how Simon had felt last night. Yes, it would have been Kevin's fault, but that didn't mean Gal and the other pride members should be as cruel as Kevin had been.

It wasn't Simon's decision to make, though, and the only thing he could do was trust that Gal knew what he was doing as the alpha. He'd been an alpha for a long time, even though he hadn't always worked with the pride, and it probably wasn't the first time he had to deal with this kind of situation.

Simon smiled at yet another pride member, who grinned at him and wiggled his eyebrows. Simon shook his head, but he was amused.

"They all noticed we're mates and bonded?" Val asked.

"That would be because your shirt is still open and they can see the mark on your neck."

Val grinned, and Simon knew he was doing it on purpose. "I'm sorry. Do you want me to close the other buttons? I would be uncomfortable, but I'll do it."

Simon rolled his eyes. "You're really proud of the fact that we're bonded, aren't you?"

"Why shouldn't I be? I'm bonded to the most perfect man in the world. I'm proud of being your mate."

Hearing Val talk this way always made Simon feel flustered, and today wasn't any different. "I'm not perfect."

"I said the most perfect man in the world, but I meant for me. You wouldn't be my mate otherwise."

That much was true. They were mates because they fit perfectly together, even though it would still take work and compromises. Simon didn't mind, though. He knew that he and Val would be together for the rest of their lives, and it was a long time. They would fight and make up. They would disagree on some things and agree on others. They would find a way to work together, just like every other couple did.

They were still in the honeymoon phase, but it wouldn't last forever. Their relationship and love for each other would, though, and Simon found himself thinking about the future. He and Val were both young, and he couldn't help but wonder if Val had ever thought about having children. Simon hadn't, mostly because he hadn't thought he would have the possibility. Until recently, he'd been a prisoner in the pride. He wouldn't have been able to get married to a man he loved, to adopt children from outside of the pride. Alpha Carter wouldn't have allowed that to happen. Simon hadn't been about to marry a woman, even a pride member, and there was no one he loved that way. He knew all the pride members, and he loved them like family, not in the way he should love a wife.

But now he wouldn't have to marry a woman, and he had the possibility of becoming a father. He couldn't make the decision on his own, and it was way too soon to talk about it, but he put it away in his brain, knowing that he would get back to it—loving that he had the possibility of coming back to it.

He and Val walked into the kitchen, and Simon froze. Kevin was there, putting together a sandwich. Simon didn't think he'd ever seen Kevin looking this down, and to his own surprise, he wanted to do something to help. He stepped closer, fully expecting Kevin to look up and see him, to repeat the things he'd been saying for so long, but instead, his eyes widened and he took a step back.

Simon stopped moving again. They stared at each other for a few moments, then, to Simon's surprise, Kevin snatched his sandwich from the counter and scurried away. He didn't say a word, even though Simon could see that he wanted to. His gaze had burned with hate, and while Simon didn't like anyone feeling that way toward him, he knew he had to wrap his mind around it. Kevin would never like him. If he stayed with the pride, Simon had to be aware that.

"I didn't think he would still be around this morning," Val said.

Simon shook his head. "I don't know what happened." But since Gal and Liam were sitting at the table, they would find out.

Simon made a beeline for them, interrupting their conversation. He didn't ask anything, just stood there, wondering how to ask. He didn't want to look like he was demanding answers from the alpha, even though that was what he wanted to do.

"We just saw Kevin," Val said, breaking the silence and taking the decision out of Simon's hands.

Gal slowly nodded. "You did. I didn't kick him out."

"Why not? You know what he did and what he said to Simon." Val sounded like he was gearing up for a fight, but Simon didn't want that to happen. He pressed a hand on Val's back, hoping it would be enough to soothe him and calm him down a little.

Gal cleaned his mouth with a napkin and leaned back in his chair. "It wasn't an easy decision to make, especially since he'd already been warned of what would happen if he continued with his behavior. We talked, though, and I agreed to give him one more chance. If he does something he shouldn't, though, he'll be out."

"You're going to allow him to hurt someone else just because you want to give him another chance?" Val asked.

Simon swallowed, unsure of how Gal would react. To his relief, Gal didn't seem offended at the way Val was talking to him.

"I'm going to keep a special eye on him, and I won't be the only one. We'll make sure he doesn't hurt anyone the way he hurt Simon. Don't worry. It's his last chance, and he knows he can't fuck it up."

Val didn't seem convinced, but Simon was okay with it. "Thank you," he said.

Gal turned his attention to him. "I should have done something sooner. I should have known this was happening. It's my job."

"Actually, it's Forest's. He's the one who deals with the pride members."

Gal shook his head. "That doesn't mean anything. Even though he's helping me, I'm still the alpha. I should know about these things."

"And I didn't tell you because you were already busy enough as it was. No matter how much you try to forget that, you haven't been our alpha for long. You're still working on building relationships with nearby prides and shifter groups and protecting the pride. *That* is the most important thing for you to do right now. Everything else can come later, once you're sure the pride is safe. I'm not angry at you for allowing Kevin to stay. Hell, I was the one who kept it from you. I probably shouldn't have, but I did, because I didn't want to burden you. I don't regret it, either, and I don't regret the fact that you allowed Kevin to stay."

Gal cocked his head. "You don't?"

"I don't. I can't say we'll ever be best friends or even friendly, but I don't want him to be alone. No matter how bad his behavior was, we've all been through a lot. We weren't allowed to leave the house, to have friends, to build relationships with people. He did what he had to do to defend himself and to survive." And until Alpha Carter and Beta Boyd had left, it had worked. Kevin had stood up to them, albeit only marginally, and he'd managed to build a life for himself with the pride.

Things were different now, though. Alpha Carter and Beta Boyd were gone, and Kevin had to get used to the new pride. If he couldn't do that, well, he wouldn't be a part of it for long. Simon hoped that wouldn't happen. It might make him an idiot, but he didn't want Kevin to suffer. Yes, he'd behaved badly, but Simon understood, at least in part.

"Why don't you sit down and have breakfast with us?" Liam said, gesturing at the empty seats at the table.

"We should probably talk about the two of you," Gal agreed.

Val sat in front of Gal and stared at him. "I want Simon to move in with me in town."

Simon sucked in a breath. He hadn't expected Val to be so straight to the point, and he didn't know what to do now.

He released his breath when Gal just nodded. "I thought something like that would happen. Let us know if you need help moving, Simon."

Simon blinked at him. "You mean you don't want us to stay here with the pride?"

"You'll always be a pride member, as long as you want to be one. But no, you don't have to live with us. You won't be far anyway. I think it'll be a good thing for you and Val to have your own life in your own home. I don't expect any of the pride members to stick around, not if they don't want to. You're all free to move into town, get your own house, your own life. The pack will always be here for you because we're family, but I won't clip your wings the way Alpha Carter did. You're free to go, Simon."

Simon was free. It was hard to believe, but he was, and he knew he would never lose this. It wasn't only because of Gal, either. With Alpha Carter gone, Simon had allowed himself to fall in love with Val and hoped he would have a life.

He did now.

You may also enjoy the following from eXtasy Books Inc:

Leap of Faith
Catherine Lievens

Excerpt

Peter was sitting on a short half wall on the other side of the street from his building, staring at his phone, when Emily called him back. He continued staring, wary of answering. For whatever reason, he didn't want to know what she was about to tell him.

He'd panicked when he'd called her earlier. He didn't have a lot of friends—actually, he didn't have any friends. He had people he was friendly with, but he knew he couldn't call them and ask them for a place to stay or a job. His sister, on the other hand, was his sister. They'd grown up together, and they'd always been close. He'd hoped she could help him, at least with a place for the night, but now, he was afraid to answer in case she couldn't.

What would he do if she couldn't help him? Where would he spend the night? He had some savings, so he could get a hotel, but it wouldn't last long. He also had to find a job, and he didn't know where to start, not with his personal computer and everything else under water in his apartment.

It hadn't only flooded. The pipe had exploded right in Peter's living room. The pressure had destroyed the wall, and from what he'd been told, it had ruined everything that had been in there. He hadn't seen the place yet because the firefighters hadn't allowed him inside, but he already knew from the way they looked at him with pity that there wouldn't be a lot he could save. That was yet another problem, and a problem he didn't know how to solve.

He sucked in a breath and answered. "Please tell me you found a couch on which I can sleep tonight."

"I did better than that. I found you a job and a bedroom in which you can stay for as long as you need to."

Peter was relieved for all of five seconds. Then, he narrowed his eyes. "That sounds too good to be true. What are the conditions?"

"No conditions. It's not in Boston, though. You're going to have to move."

Peter close his eyes and swallowed. It was better than he'd expected. It wasn't like he loved living here anyway. He was here because it was where he'd gone to college and where he'd found his first job, and he'd stayed here because, well, it was what he knew and what he'd known for the past several years. He didn't have family, though. Emily had moved when she'd graduated and was working in another city.

What would Peter be leaving behind if he left? Not much — a flooded apartment, a job he'd just lost. He had a few friends he would miss, but that was it.

He sighed. "Tell me."

"I called Sean."

Peter rolled his eyes. "Of course you did." Emily and Sean had been best friends since college, and they were so close that Peter had always wondered if there was more between them than friendship. He'd never met Sean, though. Their schedule had never fit together when Sean and Emily had been in college, and that was fine. Or at least, it had been fine until now. Since it seemed that Sean was giving Peter everything he needed, though, he wished he knew him better.

"Who else did you expect me to call?" Emily asked. "He's always been there when I'm I was trouble, and today isn't any different. He's offering you his guest room and a job. It won't be as an accountant, though."

Peter bit his lower lip. "What kind of job is he offering, then?"

"He owns a construction company. Most of his family is in that kind of job. His father was before him, and one of his brothers builds furniture."

"Construction? Can you imagine me working in construction?"

"I can't, but it's the only thing he has available. You can say no if you want, Peter. I did what I could, but I understand it's not what you expected."

Peter couldn't say no. He didn't want to sound ungrateful, but more importantly, he couldn't afford to. He needed a job and a place to stay, and this was the easiest way to get that. He felt slightly guilty — he was an adult, and he should be able to find a job on his own. He was down on his luck, though, and he felt like he was drowning along with all this stuff. He needed help, no matter how little he liked admitting it. He liked even less that Emily had called Sean to get that help, but really, he should have guessed she would. She always called Sean when she had a problem, and this time hadn't been any difference.

"It will help you get back on your feet," Emily murmured. "He's a good man, Peter. I know you don't know him and that you're slightly wary of him, but I promise you that he'll do everything he can for you."

"I don't understand why," Peter admitted.

"He's not like us, like our family. I know we've always had each other's back, but it's only us. Sean has a big family, though. He has six brothers, and they've always been there for each other, as did their parents. I'm part of his family, too, which means he'll do everything he can to help me, and through me, you."

"Even though he doesn't know me?"

"I vouched for you. He trusts me. He wants to help me. Allow him to do that, please. I don't know who else to call. I want to do what I can for you, but I don't think there's anything else in my power."

Peter couldn't say no. "I'll go."

Emily sounded relieved. "Good. I'll text you his address and his phone number. He expects a call from you."

"How far does he live?"

"I'm guessing it's going to take you four or five by car. That's how long it took him to go home for the holidays and stuff when we were in college. You still have your car, do you?"

"That's the only thing I still have." Peter regretted his words right away. With how his life was going, it was going to break down or something like that.

"All right. See what you can save from your apartment and go to Sean."

"Thank you."

"You don't have to thank me. We're family."

That much was true. He and Emily were closer now than they'd been as children, and while she'd been the only one Peter could call for help, he hadn't truly expected her to do this. Instead, she'd found him a place to stay and a job. He didn't care if he had to build walls or something like that. He would do what he had to do to survive.

They hung up, and a few seconds later, his phone trilled with a text. It was the information Emily had promised to send, and Peter stared at the address on the screen.

Emily had been right. It was going to take him at least five hours to drive there. It was a small town, too, so it would be a change of scenery. Maybe that was what he needed. Living in the city on his own hadn't worked. None of it was his fault, but he had a chance at a new start, and he wanted to take it.

He got to his feet and looked at the building, then at the

firefighters still milling around. He needed to grab the few things that had survived the flooding—if anything had—and then, he would leave. He had to talk to the firefighters. They wouldn't let him inside on his own, and he understood why. He wanted to leave all of this behind, and the sooner he did it, the better it would be. His life had flipped upside down in one afternoon, and he was lost. He didn't know if he would be able to find a way forward, but Emily's help had been a good start. He didn't have anything to stay for, but a lot to leave behind.

About the Author

Catherine is the creator of several series, most of them paranormal, including the Whitedell Pride Series and the Gillham Pack Series. While she graduated in translation, she decided to go the writer's way because it was more fun to create her own stories and characters.

She's been living in Italy for more than twenty years, but she's a daughter of the North—Belgium to be precise—and she misses it so much that she's already planning to move back.

She loves pizza—probably too much—her son, her pets, and of course, books. She sneaks some reading time into her schedule every time she has five minutes free from writing, demands from her various pets and son, and lastly, housework.

Connect with her:

lievens.catherine@gmail.com
BookBub: https://www.bookbub.com/authors/catherine-lievens
Website: https://authorcatherinelievens.com/
Facebook: https://www.facebook.com/catherine.lievens.9
Facebook Group: https://www.facebook.com/groups/411788002341528/
Twitter: https://twitter.com/authorCLievens
Newsletter: http://eepurl.com/c-uvKn

www.ingramcontent.com/pod-product-compliance
Lightning Source LLC
Chambersburg PA
CBHW060631130626
46555CB00002B/750